PRAISE FOR *BIG FAN*

"It sparkles with wit—pair it with a good glass of prosecco and prepare to get lost in this smart, sexy novel."

—Elissa Sussman, bestselling author of
Once More with Feeling and *Funny You Should Ask*

T0182641

Big Fan

ALEXANDRA ROMANOFF

831 STORIES

831 Stories

An imprint of Authors Equity
1123 Broadway, Suite 1008
New York, New York 10010

Cover design by C47.
Book design by Scribe Inc.
This is a work of fiction. Names, characters, places and incidents either
are products of the author's imagination or are used fictitiously.

Library of Congress Control Number: 2024938950
Print ISBN 9798893310146
Ebook ISBN 9798893310191

Printed in the United States of America

www.831stories.com
www.authorsequity.com

Big Fan

I

Denizen looks like something out of a romance novel tonight. All around me, candles flicker on tables set with clean white linen, and bouquets of lilies bloom in their vases. It's still early, so it's not busy yet. From my seat at the bar, I can half-hear the murmured conversation of a nearby couple. The rumble of his laugh, and the way she sighs when he reaches for her hand.

I take a deep breath and try to block it all out. I only have a few minutes before I need to leave, and I want to finish reading this article before I do. *Universal basic income has been shown by multiple studies to be one of the most effective ways to relieve poverty and keep people from falling into unsheltered homelessness*, I recite to myself. *Giving people a small monthly stipend to spend however they want—on whatever they need—is cheaper and more efficient than almost any other method of combating poverty.*

The odds of anyone wanting to talk about UBI at Lana Winthrop's birthday party tonight are extraordinarily low. There will be plenty of policymakers and lobbyists there—Lana is the prom queen of the high school cafeteria that is Washington, DC. But no one comes to her parties to do business. They'll be in full-on gossip mode, busy sussing out who's hooking up with who and who's thinking of leaving their job. Who has the good drugs. And who they'll tell if you ask them to share.

I get it. I do. I used to enjoy the social speculation of these evenings. Before I became one of the unwilling subjects.

I glance at the time. Guess I can't put it off any longer. I catch Greta's eye across the bar and signal that it's time for me to close out.

"You're not staying for dinner?" she asks, sliding me my check. "We got some branzino in this morning."

"I wish. Work plans."

"Sucker," she says, but she's smiling as she leaves me to my tip math.

After my divorce, most restaurants in DC felt tainted—either they were places Cooper and I had frequented together or the waitstaff didn't bother to hide their glee at seeing the city's most famously single woman out on the town and all alone. Denizen was the exception: no one here has ever treated me like anything other than a run-of-the-mill customer. Which is what I ache to be.

The good news about Lana's party is that it's being held in my new neighborhood—right off the water at the fancy Thompson hotel in the Navy Yard. Which means that when I inevitably have to flee, it'll at least be a quick trip home.

The bad news is that it's freezing outside—much chillier than it should be in April. My cold intolerance was a minor but real source of friction in my former marriage: Cooper, who'd gone to boarding school in New Hampshire, never could get over my Southern California–tuned internal thermostat. Of course, then we ended up having bigger problems. Like his inability to keep his dick in his khakis in the presence of a pretty twenty-two-year-old.

I feel seasick at the thought of him. Nauseated and off-balance. Some small part of me always knew he wasn't the kindest guy in the world, but I never expected him to blow up both of our lives. At least I have assurance he won't be in attendance tonight: according to his Instagram, he's in New York, working on some "exciting new projects!" Gross.

When I make it to the hotel, I pause outside for a minute to gather myself. Take a few deep, crisp breaths, temperature be damned. I don't have to stay forever. I just have to make an appearance.

Then I push inside and walk as confidently as I can across the lobby, head held high. I'm alone in the elevator as it whisks me up, but as soon as the doors open onto the rooftop bar, I hear the din of a party in full swing. I slip off my trench, trading it for a coat check tag before turning to face the room.

And there it is, that moment that I always have lately, when I feel suddenly and horribly exposed. I went as prim as possible with my look, settling on a crew-neck dress with bracelet-length sleeves and an A-line skirt that makes me look something like the demure political wife I so recently was. A breeze brushes against my wrists and my ankles, stirring my hair, holding strong in a three-day-old blowout, against my collarbones and the back of my neck. I shiver at the contact.

I've been here thirty seconds and I need a drink already. I snag a glass of champagne off a passing tray, nodding my thanks to the waiter who's carrying it. I always feel such a strange double consciousness at parties like this one, which is supposed to be populated by bleeding-heart liberals . . . who somehow don't mind that everyone attending the party is white, while everyone working it isn't.

Not that this stops me from coming myself. I'm no better than the rest of them, really.

I need to find our hostess before she's too swamped; I want to make sure I get points for having shown up. But that plan is immediately disrupted by Ramona Dietrich grabbing my arm with one spidery hand. "Maya!" she cries. "Oh my god, it's been *ages.*"

Subtext: *You really went into hiding after your husband cheating on you with a campaign intern—on a senator's desk, no less—made the front page of the* Washington Post, *didn't you?*

I'm instantly grateful to have been in DC as long as I have. Succeeding in this town requires you to make nice with people way more repulsive than Ramona, and my poker face is exquisite.

I still can't keep myself from taking a shot right back at her. "A long time," I agree. "Work kept me so busy last year. It was weeks after the election before I even started to decompress. But every time I see President Knight in the White House, I know it was worth it." I flash her a big, empty smile that does not reach my eyes.

Subtext: *My candidate is now POTUS, and don't you forget it. I may be social roadkill, but as a political consultant, I'm still at the top of my game.*

"Well, you look fantastic." She gives me a smug grin, like she's scored a direct hit. In my next life, I'm going to pick a career that allows me to live in a city where that sentence doesn't double as an insult.

I started working in politics when I was young—too young to understand how careful I needed to be about being a pretty girl in rooms full of older men. Growing up the daughter of a pair of professors in San Diego didn't expose me to much business casual, and at first, I didn't understand why people here considered my linen dresses and vintage button-downs any different from their Ann Taylor Loft looks. I learned the hard way that standing out was a death sentence—but not before far too many people decided I was making professional headway because of my legs and not because I can run circles around most strategists in this city.

And, to make matters worse, I went and married into—and then, dramatically, cast myself out of—a storied political dynasty.

"She does look fantastic, doesn't she?" someone says behind me. I could die of gratitude when I turn around and see Gabe Perez. Gabe and I have known each other since college. We have approximately the same bullshit tolerance, and I know he's swooped in specifically to rescue me from Ramona.

But she's not done with me yet. "It's no surprise she got that *Vogue* profile, you little fashion plate, you."

Barely even subtext: *You're unserious.*

As if I haven't heard *that* one before. Still, it gets right under my skin and lodges there like a splinter. My hands move to smooth my hair before I can stop them. Ramona notices, and I hate that she knows she got to me.

Gabe takes an almost imperceptible step closer. His family is Argentinian, and being brown-skinned in lily-white DC has taught him plenty of lessons about how to hold his ground. "I'm pretty sure Maya was the first person to sneak a cogent description of how the debt ceiling works into those pages," he says. "Anyway, Mona, how's life in the minority leader's office lately?"

If I could applaud, I would. The election that vaulted Senator Knight into the presidency also flipped the House blue, which means that Ramona's boss is no longer top dog. And if there's one thing that Ramona Dietrich lives for, it is her status. Which has recently taken almost as big a blow as my reputation.

"Oh, you know, busy as always," she says airily. "Anyway, I think I see Leo over there—if you'll excuse me."

She's gone, and I'm not sure if I'm holding back laughter or tears. "Thank you," I say, clutching Gabe's lapels like a lifeline. "I'm so happy you're here. I thought you and Aaron were supposed to be—"

"We *were*," he says. "But we broke up a few weeks ago, so instead of vacationing in the Maldives with him, here I am." He does a little jazz-hands flourish.

"I'm sorry. I liked him."

"I liked him too. He didn't like how much I worked."

I make a sympathetic face. It's a complaint I know all too well.

The two of us pull away from the crowd, toward the edge of the roof. The sun is still up—a minor miracle, after what felt like an endless winter—and the Potomac glitters. The cherry blossoms are thick on the trees below us, and for a moment, I remember why I fell in love with DC. How romantic this city used to seem.

"How are you doing?" Gabe says after a beat.

I know what he's really asking. I would lie to anyone else here, but I trust him enough to be unvarnished. "Shitty," I say. "Coop dumped Cassidy"—The Other Woman—"and now he has some new girlfriend, and I keep seeing DeuxMoi stuff about them out together. Meanwhile, I didn't button my shirt up to the neck the other day, and the headline was about 'flashing my revenge body.'" I tug at a sleeve. "But honestly, the worst part is trying to figure out work. I *should* be able to do whatever I want right now, I should be fighting off offers with a stick! And instead, I feel like everyone is kind of keeping me at arm's length. Like, they want to work with me in theory . . . but no one can commit to a political consultant who could end up becoming the story again."

Gabe sighs and rubs my back. He's exactly as handsome as he was when we were eighteen, his dark hair still thick, and his brows expressive. But it's been seventeen long years since then, and it shows on both of our faces: the toll this town has taken on us. "They're stupid."

"And spineless."

"Do you have something specific in mind? Or are you just kind of seeing what's out there?"

I look out over the water. Coop was an accomplished sailor, and being on the water was one thing we could always agree on. I wish I was out there now, wind ruffling my hair and brine thick in my nostrils. Instead, I'm trapped high up in the sky with a bunch of people who think they rule the world. The worst part is, they're not entirely wrong.

"I've been digging into universal basic income," I confess. "It came up during Knight's campaign—one of his economic advisors knew I was interested in poverty relief." OK, *interested* is maybe an understatement. By that point, I was verging on fixated. There's only so much time you can spend grappling with people's problems in this country—the credit-card and medical debt, the crazy rents, and the jobs people work just to try to survive—without recognizing that *not enough money* is their common root. "Anyway, he passed me some of the more recent studies on it. We both knew Knight was never going to go for it. But the dream would be to push something in that direction. What about you? How are things with Powell?"

Teresa Powell had been a rising star in the House for the last few terms, and now she's running to be the governor of Massachusetts in a special election. Gabe was one of her first campaign hires, and he's been so busy since taking the job, we've barely gotten to talk.

"It's a good gig. The guy she's up against is fairly moderate, and she's looking for something that can position her as more progressive. I have no idea if she'd say yes, but . . . would you want to make a UBI pitch to her?"

A *zing* goes down my spine, and I stand up straighter. I may look like a lamb, but I'm just as sharky as everyone else in this room when it comes down to it. And I recognize a rare opportunity when it propositions me at a party. "Yes," I say. "Absolutely. If she's open to it, I'm in."

"I'll talk to her about it," he says and eyes my glass. "Time for round two?"

"Definitely time for round two."

Gabe knows exactly how to find tipsy without getting drunk, but by the time I get home, I am dying for a glass of water. As I stand in the kitchen, sipping, my gaze falls to the copy of *Vogue*

on my kitchen table. Almost automatically, I start leafing through it, landing in the spot where it's creased from having undergone this routine before: the page that features the absurdly handsome face of Charlie Blake.

My first celebrity crush, and also something like my political origin story—in the mid-'90s, I was so obsessed with Charlie's boy band, Mischief, that my best friend Kate and I helped start one of their first national fan clubs as fifteen-year-olds. The club, Making Mischief, introduced me to the power of organizing— and my own powers of persuasion.

I always bring this up in interviews when I can. Because I think it's a good reminder that the passions of young girls are worth nurturing no matter how frivolous they may seem . . . and also because someday Mischief is going to do a reunion tour, and I'd like access to good tickets. One of the first rules of being a political operative: know who to flatter to get what you want.

Usually, though, we're not being featured in the same issue of the same publication. Charlie's spread features him modeling clothes from his own line, Char. Apparently it was just acquired by Kering, which means he's gone from extremely rich to obscenely wealthy.

Also obscene: the way he looks. At seventeen and eighteen, he was a rangy kid with surprisingly broad shoulders and a wicked dimpled grin. Now he's thirty-seven and filled out with muscle, crow's-feet winking at the corner of each eye. His hair is still silky, but it's dirty blond threaded with the barest hints of silver. And his hands: he has *good* hands, long fingered where they rest against a Hadid's slender shoulder.

In one image, his arms are raised over his head, and his shirt has ridden up to reveal the cut of his hip bone, the faintest hint of a happy trail below his navel. I barely remember what it feels like to have sex—to even *want* to have sex with someone—but this is starting to refresh my memory.

Charlie hasn't done an interview in almost five years, since the *New York Times* profile he sat for when Char launched. He's less reclusive than, say, Mary-Kate and Ashley, the career counterparts to whom he is frequently compared—he goes to enough Fashion Week events, and occasionally he'll pop up at a premiere to support a friend. But he's hardly as accessible as he was when he was eighteen and nineteen, and seemingly everywhere. Which has to have been a deliberate choice.

I'm surprised that I'm still so curious about what he's thinking. What's going on behind the deep green of his eyes. His role in Mischief was The Artistic One: the creative soul of the group. Fans scrutinized the books he carried with him on tour, and interviewers made note of the fact that he was self-taught on both piano and guitar. How much of that was true, I wonder. Does he miss music? Does he still make it in private?

I pull myself out of my daze and pick up my phone. I have an email from Gabe, introducing me to Representative Powell's secretary so we can set a meeting for next week. Right. I'm a grown-up person, with a real life. I toss the magazine on a stack with my other mail, take a last sip of water, and start to get myself ready for bed.

II

Representative Powell's DC campaign office is in a nondescript building, but I recognize the energy as soon as I walk in. It's the scent of stale coffee and days-old takeout, and the way sleepless-ness and anxiety are thick in the air. There's nubby, ugly carpeting under my feet and buzzing fluorescents overhead, but still, my heart rate kicks up a notch, adrenaline spiking in anticipation. I'm not in the habit of quoting *Hamilton*, but this *is* one of the rooms where it happens. And this is the energy that's kept me from leaving politics, even when staying starts to feel like self-sabotage.

Everyone who works here is set up in the main room on fold-ing tables, a few with temporary cubicle walls thrown up around them as a gesture at privacy, except Representative Powell, who has the only actual office in the space. An assistant ushers me in to see her, and then politely disappears.

Teresa Powell is fifteen or twenty years older than I am, I'd guess, a stern-looking white woman with cornsilk-blonde hair. Imposing and impressive—but both are traits I'm accustomed to by now. She's dressed in the standard-issue dark DC suit. She must have come straight from the Capitol to meet me.

"I appreciate you taking the time," I say as I pull up a seat.

"Listen, when you hear that Maya McPherson is interested in your campaign, you hear her out," Powell says, settling back in her chair. "I've been following your work for a long time now—since everything you did to get Reese Wright into the House in '12."

"That's a deep cut." It was my first big job, and I'm flattered and impressed that she knows about it.

"I do my research. Gabe said you had a specific policy idea in mind? UBI?"

Oh, thank god. This is the easy part. I nod and take a deep breath. Smile brightly. "I think it's exactly right for you. It's ambitious, it's smart, it's progressive, and with all the studies that have been done, it's defensible. Poverty is still on the rise in Massachusetts, and this is a whole new way of tackling it. I know you're running as a breath of fresh air, and Representative Powell—"

"Teresa," she corrects me.

"Teresa. *This* would be fresh. UBI has never been piloted across a whole state. I think that, with the right framing, you could make the case, and I can help you make it."

She's been sizing me up while I'm talking, and when I finish, she nods once, just slightly, to herself, like I've passed some kind of test. "Let me talk to my economic advisors," she says. "But I'm fairly well-versed on the concept and generally open to it. I did want to ask you something else, though. Are you sure *you're* the right person to be making this argument? Now?"

At first I'm confused—what about me seems ill-suited to make the case for UBI? I have no wealth to hoard even if I wanted to, no offshore bank accounts to speak of. My parents are comfortable, but you don't have to have experienced poverty to be sympathetic toward it . . . and then I realize what she's actually asking. Teresa is raising the distraction question—wondering if my reputation will get in the way.

I knew it was coming, but that doesn't make it any less painful to actually be asked. The acid burn of shame rises in my throat. My job is to control the story, and usually, I'm so good at it. I still don't understand how I ended up . . . here.

I take a deep breath. Make deliberate eye contact. Force myself to calmly recite the speech I've practiced. "I'm aware that my name comes with certain . . . associations. But Cooper's affair broke in the middle of President Knight's campaign, and we still managed to pull out a win. I do know how to shift the spotlight when it's necessary and how to keep attention where it needs to be."

I try to read her face. Did I strike the right tone? Clear but not confrontational? Neither automaton nor trainwreck? I realize in that moment how much I want this, and not just for the platform. My bank account is hanging in there for now, but I do actually need steady income if I'm going to keep paying rent on a one-bedroom in the District.

I'm so focused on nailing my pitch that I almost forget to be angry about having to defend myself for being cheated on. During a job interview.

Teresa nods thoughtfully. "I'm not questioning your work," she says. "But Maya, you and I both know how it is for women, especially in this town. Even if you keep your head down, you can't guarantee what the press will decide to pick up."

She's right, of course. I know it better than anyone. Better than her even. "Ultimately, it's up to you whether you think I'm a risk worth taking. But like you said, I do have some experience with this. I can't answer for my ex-husband, and I can't make promises about anyone else's behavior. But my track record speaks for itself."

Teresa moves on to other questions. I cite Stanford and McKinsey studies; I share food security and child poverty data, and I know I sound competent and smart. But I spend the rest of the conversation with a bitter aftertaste in the back of my throat. My track record *should* speak for itself. My measured silence for months, paired with my sincere, carefully worded quotes in *Vogue*—they should have put a lid on this already. How is it not enough to convince anyone that I didn't want this attention?

But rage won't help me get a job. So I swallow it as best I can and smile until my cheeks ache. I need Teresa to hire me. Because if another woman won't take a chance on me, who will?

I can't bear the idea of going home to my soulless, empty apartment, so after I leave Teresa, I head to a bar down the block. It's pretty standard: dark wood, brass fixtures, political memorabilia on the walls. It's only 3:00 p.m., but I order a martini anyway and spend a few minutes luxuriating in the sharp taste of gin and lemon. Someday, this part of my life will be a long time ago.

But we're not there yet. So I give in to the inevitable and start going through the emails I missed while Teresa and I were talking. If there's one constant in my life—through my marriage, its spectacular end, and all of the aftermath—it's the flood of fundraising emails from campaigns I've never heard of and media inquiries from journalists I'll never talk to. "Just thinking of you!" missives from women I haven't spoken to since grade school. Every graduating senior in the DMV area wants to "pick my brain." I delete, delete, delete so fast that I almost miss a subject line that says *Request from Charlie Blake*.

The body reads,

Hi Maya! I'm reaching out on behalf of Charlie Blake—he loved the way you talked about Mischief in your *Vogue* interview and was excited about your resume and your connection to his career. Charlie is launching a new project and was hoping to discuss having you come on to consult. It's still in stealth mode, so I've attached an NDA for you to sign. Once it's returned, I'd love to catch you up on details and connect you with Charlie. Let me know if you're interested and available!

Very best,

Merrill

I finish the rest of my martini in a single swallow. It burns going down, and the letters on my screen swim briefly in front of my eyes. But I blink, and there they are again: those same sentences, in that same order.

Holy fucking shit.

My fingers navigate to my contacts without any conscious input from me. Since I was fifteen, I have done the same thing every time I was excited about something, especially anything Mischief-related, which is "call Kate and yell." And that's exactly what I'm about to do when the bartender interrupts me. He must have noticed my suddenly empty glass. "Another one?" he asks.

I don't trust my voice. I just shake my head no.

God, I don't think I can even talk to Kate about this. Because she's going to hype me up. And I need to be rational. I need to be smart. I think I need to say no.

Because I know what this is. I get this kind of ask occasionally—celebrities want to launch charities, and they want me to come sit on their board or rally advisors to make whatever they're doing look legit. The causes are as softball as it gets: they feed poor kids the occasional lunch or take veterans to baseball games. Nice gestures, but they never make any kind of meaningful change in the world. Merrill must have seen me giving Mischief airtime and thought, *Oooh, Maya McPherson, she'll be easy. Bet she's desperate for a gig. Maybe we can get her for cheap.*

The thought makes me feel tired, and sad. The bar back is mirrored, and I catch my own reflection in it. I run a hand through my auburn hair, and it still falls flat. I had put on my best professional face to meet up with Teresa, but underneath the makeup, I look pale and sour. All these years of working in politics, but nothing has made me as cynical as the last fifteen months.

When I was fourteen, Mischief made the world feel worth living in. I would stare out the windows of my middle school and daydream about meeting them, and how, when I did, everything would change. I'd go on tour and see the world. Become friends with fashion designers and get dressed in fabulous clothes. Mischief was proof that something bigger and more important than eighth-grade formal existed, and eventually I'd get to be a part of it. I used to think my life would really start the day Charlie Blake knew my name.

And now he does, which is funny, because up until fairly recently, I was pretty sure my life was over.

Even as I grew out of the fantasy stage, Mischief remained important to me all through high school, and college, and after. They connected me to Kate, and together, we created a community of girls who were just as passionate as we were. I can still tap the thrill of mobilizing a massive group of fans, the awe I felt watching how infectious and powerful our enthusiasm was. Mischief's music was a perpetual soundtrack throughout my formative years—playing when I drove a car by myself for the first time, when I collapsed into my bed after my first breakup, and when I got on the plane to head to college. Cooper tried to convince me not to, but I snuck one of their songs onto the playlist for our wedding reception. That band—their music—sits at the gooiest, most intimate center of myself.

If the email was from anyone else, I would ignore it. But I obviously can't just click *delete*. So I write back with my phone number, knowing that I'm being silly. Charlie doesn't care about this enough to chase me down. But just in case he does, well, he's welcome to contact me directly.

III

Teresa doesn't keep me hanging. The next afternoon, she calls with good news. Her voice is warm and welcoming when she says, "I know we can do great things together." *Phew*, I think. *I passed.*

"I can't wait to come on board."

"Well, I appreciate your enthusiasm," she says. "But."

My heart stutters, and my smile dies on my lips.

"Senator Knight had a long history in politics; my name won't get us as far if you pull focus. So I do want you to keep a low profile during this campaign."

I close my eyes. I mean, Cooper can't exactly leave me again. But there's no point in being sharp. Especially before I've even signed a contract. So I exhale the words, unsaid. "That's the plan," I agree, as cheerfully as I can.

After we hang up, I see a text from Gabe: *Yayyyyy can't wait to be colleagues!! Let's get a drink and celebrate later?*

I don't respond right away. I know I should be thrilled, and I am, mostly. But there's also a knot of dread in my stomach: a fear that I will fuck this up, and then I'll never be hirable again. I focus on the rise and fall of my chest. Try to clear my mind of the dark thoughts. Finally, I write back, *Of course! Where's the happy hour spot near the office? IOU at least two rounds.*

Coming into campaigns late is always challenging, and I spend the first week playing frantic catch-up: learning names and roles, ingratiating myself with advisors, trying to figure out who says they'll make things happen and who actually does. I reward myself for making it through with an 8:00 p.m. Pilates class on Friday—the last one on the schedule for the day. It's good to get out of my head and into my body. To be reminded that I *have* a body, something I've found myself trying to forget for the last year or so.

I'm walking through the front door of my apartment building when my phone starts ringing in my bag, and I jam the volume bar down so that it will go silent again. The call is from an unknown number. Spam.

Once I'm in my apartment, rinsed off and wearing sweatpants, I go into the kitchen to try to figure out if I have the energy to make dinner or if I'm ordering takeout again. I'm plugging my phone into a speaker when I realize that same number called again. And then sent a text.

It's from *Maybe: Charlie Blake.*

I drop my phone.

I have to take a lap around the room before I can pick it up again. Whatever composure I thought I had developed in the decades—decades!—since I was fourteen absolutely deserts me, and all I can feel is my heart fizzing like soda water in my chest. *Charlie Blake Charlie Blake Charlie Blake Charlie Blake!*

I sit down on the floor next to the phone, leaning back against the cabinets. They're flimsy like everything in the overpriced new build I moved into when I was still delirious with divorce grief. My hands are shaking.

OK. OK. I'm a grown-up.

If this is some mass text thing—*I'm Charlie Blake, and I'm urging you to save the whales*—I am going to feel *very* silly.

I open it. And it is not a mass text.

Hey—this is Charlie Blake. Merrill said you wanted to talk, so . . . can we talk?

I'm actually in DC tonight. Can I buy you a drink?

And then, a few minutes later: *(Is this flattering or presumptuous? I hope it's a little bit flattering.)*

I stand up, put my phone on the counter. Open the fridge. Close it again.

The only coherent thought I can muster is that I haven't gotten Kate a wedding present yet. A video of Charlie congratulating her on her marriage would make her life.

It's not a good enough reason to say yes. But the thing is, in this moment, I cannot make my brain produce a single reason to say no. I mean, I'm not going to work with him—there's no way. But why can't I tell him that to his stupid, gorgeous face? Don't I deserve a little treat after all of this . . . everything?

The *Vogue* issue is still sitting on the kitchen table. I know if I opened it, it would fall open to his picture.

I haven't wanted anything except peace and quiet since the morning I saw Cooper's sexts to Cassidy in newsprint. The sense of something stirring deep within me—flint striking rock, spark licking tinder, something like desire making itself known—is enough to move me to action. I have to eat dinner anyway. Would it be so bad if he bought it for me?

I grab my phone with both hands and hit *call*.

He answers right away. Like he was waiting for me. "Hi," he says, and even though we're not in the same room, I feel his voice like it's dripping down my spine.

"It's both flattering and presumptuous," I say before I think. "Audacious, maybe, is the right word for it."

"Could be worse," he says. "You calling me is a good sign."

"So, I could do drinks. But there has to be food. I just worked out, and I'm starving."

I'm not doing the world's best job at sounding normal. But Charlie just laughs. It's such an easy, friendly sound. "You tell me where to meet you," he says. "I'll be there."

It's close to 9:45, which means most places are close to closing. DC is not a late-night town. But the kitchen at Denizen stays open until 11:00. A small part of me knows that bringing him to my favorite spot is a bad idea—if he disappoints me, which is likely, I'll never be able to go back there and have it feel the same. But also: I still can't think.

"I can be there in twenty," he says. "Want me to call you a car?"

I shake my head before I remember he can't see me. "No. I'll walk."

"See you soon."

I barely register hanging up. My brain's moved on to figuring out what the hell to wear and trying not to spiral over the fact that I have so little time to do it. Ever since I started working in politics, I've thought of clothes as a cross between a costume and a suit of armor, and that's only been more true since the divorce.

At first, I reach for something soft—a dress. Something I might have worn on date night with Coop in another life. But this is not a date. This is business.

So I put on a pair of high-waisted, flared trousers that give me giraffe legs. At 5′8″, I'm usually careful about how much I emphasize my height—the wrong heel has me eye level with guys who swear they're six feet tall and don't want to be reminded they're not. Then I add a cream silk blouse, because I do want to look at least a little professional. Small gold hoop earrings. Hair stays up, because I did not wash it, and it shows. A swipe of lip gloss. OK.

Time to go make my dreams come true, I guess.

IV

I had figured I would have to wait for Charlie—you always have to wait for celebrities. But twenty minutes later, he's waiting for me in front of Denizen, hands shoved into the pockets of his jeans. He's wearing what I recognize to be a Char sweater and a leather jacket, and his hair catches the streetlamp's light.

My heart hiccups at the sight as my brain starts to come to terms with what's happening. I've seen him in person before, but only at concerts, and from a great distance. He's taller than I thought he would be—actual-person tall, not just famous-person tall. *I could have worn any shoes I wanted.*

This close, I can register details that *Vogue* photoshopped out of existence: the scar that runs across the top of the knuckles on his right hand, and the scuffs on his worn-in Sambas. Some celebrities look plastic up close—well-preserved but slightly waxen with the effort of it. Not Charlie. He seems like he would be soft to the touch.

Not that I'm going to touch him.

He looks up, sees me, and smiles. His lips are lush. Any plans I had to not stare at him all night fly out the window. "Maya," he says warmly. "Hey."

I nod, and he offers me his hand. I process that I'm meant to shake it and do. His grip is strong. Even after all these years, he's still got guitar-string calluses on his fingers, and whatever distant spark I felt looking at his picture bursts into flame at the contact. I imagine how they would feel against the skin of my cheeks, my hips, my breasts. I duck to hide my blush.

I'm torn between relief that I can still feel that way and mortification at my own desire. *Be professional.* Fat chance.

"It's nice to meet you," I make myself say after what feels like an awkwardly long silence.

Charlie called ahead for a table, and he must have asked for privacy, because we're seated in one of the back corners, under a shadowy little overhang. There's already a candle burning on the table, making the space cozy and intimate. God, he even smells good: the soft bloom of sandalwood and cedar, mixed with something spicy and smoky just underneath.

As I'm sliding my jacket off, I notice a woman noticing Charlie. She's my age, maybe a few years older, and I can't tell if she recognizes him or if she's just appreciating how handsome he is.

I turn away quickly so that she won't see my face. Charlie is more famous than I am by leaps and bounds, but in this town, right now, I might be more recognizable. And then I realize I haven't thought this through at all. Denizen isn't a hot spot, but it only takes one person—one photo—for this to become a story. Why did I agree to meet him in public?

Though would meeting him in private really have been better?

All of the anxiety I've been holding in for the last fifteen months rips through my bloodstream. A cold sweat seeps over my skin, and I feel clammy and dizzy.

Then Charlie says, "You know, I always thought those shirts you guys made were funny."

Excuse me, what?

"The, um, what were they?" he continues. "The *We Like to Make Mischief* ones, or something like that?"

"*I Am a Fan of Mischief*." Kate and I ran a little merch business the summer between sophomore and junior year of high school. Fan club members could mail us checks or cash—that's how long ago this was—and we would send them shirts we'd screen-printed. Mischief's official merch was hideous, so they were pretty popular. I still have one somewhere, I think. "I didn't know you guys noticed stuff like that."

"I had to look at something while we performed."

"Yeah, no, sure, I just—" I blink at this man in front of me, trying to refocus. I've never met this person, but also we have a history together. It's so strange to try to navigate. "It's nice that you remember."

Charlie shrugs adorably. "I didn't realize it at the time. But I guess I've been impressed with you for decades. Big fan."

Oh god, I'm blushing again. The waiter arrives to take our orders, and I'm grateful for the chance to get my feet under me. I have no idea what to say in response to this, so I try to get us back on track. "So tell me, what's the project?"

Charlie leans in a little bit, and I find myself doing the same. "So," he says, "I don't know how closely you've followed my career since Mischief, but I haven't been back in a recording studio since we made *Late Breaking*. After we broke up, I considered Char my creative outlet, and I thought that would be it. Like I didn't need music in that way anymore."

A lot of people were surprised when Charlie started a clothing company. But it made enough sense to me. He'd spent so many years being told what to wear; of course he wanted to be in total control of his clothing now. And the way he had talked about music—before, when he was still in the band—you could tell that he was someone who had to make stuff. Whose restless energy needed somewhere to go.

He takes a drink of his water, and I watch his throat work. Notice the tendons flexing in his forearms. It's a very casual kind of noticing, I assure myself.

"I spent this past winter hanging out with Devin at his family's farm," Charlie continues. "Devin is—" I raise an eyebrow, and he laughs. "OK, you know who Devin is. Well, then maybe you know he's had . . . kind of a hard time."

That's an understatement. During the four years they were a band, Mischief's label worked the boys to the bone. They toured and recorded, toured and recorded, in an endless loop. As soon as it ended, Ramsey did his first stint in rehab. Chris became a method actor famous for his on-set tantrums. Devin moved to a farm and took a year-long vow of silence. Apparently, he still doesn't talk much.

Even Charlie, who continues to present as the most stable one in the group, had his share of questionable girlfriends and late nights out in those early years. He's never talked about it publicly, but it was hard not to notice that behavior stopped right around Ramsey's third visit to Promises Malibu. And just a few years before he started Char.

"I try to go visit them when I can," Charlie says. "His daughter is thirteen now, and I want her to know . . . you know. To have some connection to that part of her dad's life." There's a sweetness on his face when he talks about Devin and his daughter. Something so intimate and private that I almost feel like I shouldn't be allowed to see. "Anyway, she wants to be a musician. There isn't much to do up there, and at some point, she and I started noodling around on some songs together." He fiddles with the hem of his napkin, and I'm suddenly more aware of the one I've draped across my lap. "Once we really got going, it was like something had unlocked. And all of this music that I'd been holding back for years just came tumbling out."

The waiter returns with my white wine, Charlie's old-fashioned. He lifts his glass, and I clink mine against it. His eyes stay locked with mine as we each take our first sips.

It's good luck, I think, but my body is reacting as if it's something much stronger.

"That sounds intense."

"Yeah. But . . . good intense, I think. It turned out I had a lot to say. Eventually, my therapist convinced me to get into a recording studio. He was basically like, 'You don't have to release anything, but stop being so scared of something you used to love.'"

I remember sitting in Teresa's office just last week, promising to keep my mouth shut and my head down. I nod. If Charlie can see my mind reeling, he doesn't acknowledge it. "So," he says, "it was the kick in the ass I didn't know I needed, and now I'm releasing a solo album. And I came here because I want you to help me do it."

It is very, very alluring to hear him say the words *I want you*, no matter what follows. His face is so eager and sincere, and he's so compelling and confident. And so insanely fucking handsome.

So handsome that for a moment, I forget to respond.

"Listen, I know you're beyond this," he says into my silence. "Helping a guy you were a fan of in high school with his album release. You can name your rate, and I'll—"

I have to cut this off before he says another word. "I can't. I mean, I really . . . I really can't. I just took on a new candidate. This was my first week."

"Oh, shit. Congratulations." He looks a little disappointed, but he sounds like he's actually happy for me too. Of course he is. Of course he has to look like that *and* be a genuinely decent guy too.

"But even if I hadn't—I'm a political consultant. I wouldn't know the first thing about what to do for a musician."

Charlie shakes his head emphatically. "You're a *fan*," he says. "Or you were, once. And fans are the people who made the band. *You* turned Mischief from a joke between me and my friends into something that changed my life. And I think you understand what other fans want better than I, or any record executive or social media manager, ever could."

He's looking at me now, intense and unguarded, and I feel myself getting lost in it. I want to be the person he thinks I am—the person I used to think I was. Mischief Maya had never met a mountain she couldn't move. "That was a long time ago."

Charlie holds his hands up. "I know. I know."

Our food arrives, and we busy ourselves with our silverware.

"So what's the job?" he asks just when the silence is starting to feel unbearable.

"I'm consulting for Teresa Powell—she's running for governor of Massachusetts."

"Sure, I know that name."

Charlie has been New York–based for so long, it's easy to forget that before that, he was a Boston boy.

"Why her?" he asks. "How did she win the Maya McPherson sweepstakes? People must have been throwing themselves at you after Knight's victory, right?"

I shrug. We don't need to get into why that didn't happen. "We're introducing a universal basic income platform into her campaign. They did a pilot in Boston a few years ago—giving a five-hundred-dollar monthly stipend to people, to spend however they wanted. The results were impressive, so this feels like the right time and the right person to give it some momentum."

"Oh, I know."

"You do?" As soon as I say it, I wince at myself. It's not like just because he's famous, he can't read the news.

"My mom has been a teacher in the Watertown school district for forty years. She says the guaranteed income project made the biggest difference of any of the interventions she's ever seen."

"Oh wow." The part of my brain that never stops working catalogs that I should reach out to her for a testimonial at some point.

"How did you get interested in UBI?"

"I've worked on so many campaigns over the years. I've heard a lot of candidates explain a lot of ways they're going to do something about poverty. And then, next election cycle—same poverty. Same ideas. It's exhausting. Exhausting to go meet people, and shake their hands, and smile, and promise to fix things. And to watch things stay the same."

I can feel myself picking up steam, and I know I should probably stop. But Charlie just nods, like, *Say more*. So I do.

"So many of the problems in this country stem from not being able to afford things. You can't afford fresh food, you get sick, but you can't afford a doctor, and you get sicker. You can't afford to buy things with cash, so you put it on credit and go into debt that just keeps compounding. Any assistance programs we do have—they're bureaucratic and expensive to operate. We need to cut through the red tape. We need to put a floor under people's feet. And selfishly, I need to feel like all the bullshit I put up with—that it actually means something."

"That's it!" Charlie's eyes somehow get even greener when he's excited. "That's like, exactly it. Obviously making an album isn't like, the same as what you're doing at all. I'm sorry I'm even comparing them. But that's so much of what I want: to make the stuff with Mischief—all the bullshit—lead to something meaningful."

He pauses, and I wonder if we're both thinking about his bandmates and the tailspins they have and haven't been able to pull out of. When Charlie speaks again, his voice is slower, more measured. "I was famous for no reason for so long. I sang songs that didn't matter to me and did interviews in order to say nothing. Now I would like to *say* something. To try to actually use my own voice. Or whatever." His cheeks are flushed, and I can't tell if it's from the whiskey, or the warmth of the restaurant, or just how animated he is. It's stupidly sexy.

But also: "The songs mattered to me," I remind him.

"They did," he says. "And that does mean something. It does." He gives me a heartbreaking smile, somehow happy and sad at the same time. "But I was a product, you know? It would be nice to have a chance to be an artist." Charlie is blushing up to his hairline, and I'm so charmed that I know I'm not masking it. "I know that's stupid. But I've been working on being honest about what I want, and so . . . yeah. That's it."

I think about the recent past. How once I found out my marriage was imploding, I shut down everything that wasn't required to keep me alive. How much easier it is to be a blank slate. How hard it's been to wrest myself out of stasis and start pursuing what I want again. "I think it's brave," I tell him. It comes out so soft that Charlie has to lean in a fraction of an inch closer to hear me.

Our eyes meet across the table. And for a moment, there's no one else here, anywhere. Just us and the way he looks at me, with unearned tenderness. "When we decided to stop being Mischief, it felt like the end of the world," he says. "It's taken me a long time to see that I was wrong. The world wasn't over. Just . . . different than it had been. Anyway." He tilts his head, examining me from a new angle. "Thank you. For listening."

The moment stretches out, and I feel something start to simmer between us. A hum of tension. A flicker of electricity. His eyes fall to my mouth, then rise again.

He looks away first, and my cheeks heat instantly. What *was* that? Is there any universe where he . . .

I don't have the tools to interpret this, so I don't try. I busy myself rearranging my napkin. And focus on a truth I can tell. "I loved the old songs. But I want to hear the new ones."

Charlie's grin is back, and I force myself not to imagine it pressed against my mouth. "Well, even if you're too busy for me, I can make that happen for you."

After dinner, Charlie and I stand on the sidewalk, and he turns toward me. "Even if nothing comes of this, I'm glad I came."

"I thought I gave a firm no." I'm tipsy, though it's hard to say whether it's the wine or just him.

"You did," he acknowledges. "But if you ever change your mind—or have any thoughts on . . . anything. You have my number."

For just a second, I let myself imagine that Charlie's not Charlie and I'm not me. That we're just two people saying goodnight after dinner and drinks. It's tempting to wonder if the easy way we talked—the easy way I feel when he looks at me—has legs.

But in reality, we are two people with lives pulling us in completely opposite directions. He's about to be a star again, and I'm still a walking billboard for scandal who should be avoiding anything and anyone who might be even remotely interesting to TMZ.

"It was really nice to meet you," I tell Charlie Blake, extending my hand to shake his again. And then I have to turn around and walk away before I can do anything *really* stupid, like try to hug him, to find out if he feels as good as he looks.

A few days later, I'm working late when an email from Charlie appears in my inbox. He's sent me two tracks from the album. *You said you wanted to hear it*, he's written. *So here's a taste.*

I give myself all of ten seconds to think about the corny or dirty interpretations of that wording before very deliberately finishing the task I'm working on. Then I check my email again to make sure nothing important came in while I was focusing and pack up my stuff and get ready to leave for the night. It's not outrageously late—only seven thirty, and most of the staff wrapped up a couple of hours ago. But I feel like I'm still proving myself to Teresa. Plus, there's always more work to be done.

Normally I'd take a car home and save myself the headache of navigating the metro. But I want to experience these songs while being out in the world. Maybe I'm afraid of being alone with them. I start walking to the nearest station.

I'm halfway through the first track when I realize I've been expecting something that sounds like Mischief: big anthemic stadium pop. This is quieter, richer, with instrumentation that laps around the warmth of Charlie's voice.

It's insanely good. Both of them are.

I listen again, and again, and again, while I wait for the train, while it rattles me toward home. I had forgotten what it was like to feel this way—just totally undone by someone's art, swept up in their emotions. Experiencing my own feelings as too big for my skin.

I open up my text history and tap my thumb against the screen, stalling. Charlie did tell me I could call him. He sent me these songs. It still feels crazy that I have his number. That I can just write, *These are amazing*, and then, *I love them*. And know he'll read it.

He writes back a few hours later, as I'm getting into bed. *I'm so glad. We're releasing "Longer Gone" as a single next week. Unofficially, just as a friend—do you think it's the right move?*

A friend, I repeat to myself, trying to pretend I'm not disappointed. *A friend.*

Definitely the right move, I assure him.

Three dots pop up on the screen as he types. I hold my breath, watching them and waiting. He doesn't send anything for long enough that I finally put my phone on my nightstand. I check it first thing when I wake up in the morning, but whatever he was thinking about saying, I guess he decided to keep it to himself.

V

The next few weeks are hectic. I'm helping plan for the debate where Teresa will officially announce that she's supporting UBI and the press conference that will follow the day after. When I'm not in work-mode, I'm on the phone with Kate, troubleshooting the last details of her big day.

I'm hours away from getting on a flight to LA when I take my last morning meeting before the wedding weekend. It's me, Teresa, and a bunch of junior staffers sitting around in the office, picking at cold pizza and running through details.

"OK, so we have Pastor Childress, and then Robbie Waller—the economist from Harvard," Teresa says. "Have we locked down a recipient testimonial yet?"

"We just did," one of the aides announces. "Dawson Harris. Single father; the mother died in a car accident. He works three jobs. Used the money to buy winter coats for the kids."

"We've done a background check?" Teresa asks, and the aide nods. I'm tired, and I have to bite back what I really want to say, which is that it doesn't matter if this guy has a criminal history. The *point* of UBI is that everyone deserves the dignity of being able to buy their kids winter coats. Every kid deserves to be warm in December.

But, I tell myself, Teresa is being practical. We have to convince at least some of the people for whom this isn't as obvious that it's a good idea. That's how we get her elected, and that's how this pilot gets off the ground.

"I almost want one more," Teresa adds, tapping a thoughtful finger against her chin. "Davidson"—her opponent—"just got Ben Affleck. I feel like we could use some kind of celebrity presence to help make this a little sexier. Does Chris Evans do anything antipoverty related?"

There's a clacking of keys as people start googling. Staffers throw out names and debate who might be a good ask. I'm barely listening. I don't need to ask Google anything, because I *do* know a celebrity with a connection to UBI. One who wants to use his voice more.

It's not a leap to picture Charlie on a political stage. He's so easy to talk to, and he conveys sincerity in a way that can't be taught. He made me feel like I'd known him forever, and I've never been more guarded than I am right now.

Also, this could score me such major points if it works out. "I have a connection to Charlie Blake," I say, when it's quiet enough to interject. "From the band Mischief? His mom is a teacher in Boston and apparently had students who were a part of the program there a few years ago. I could ask him if he's interested."

Teresa turns her steely-eyed gaze to one of the interns. "Does your generation know who Charlie Blake is?" she asks.

"He has that new song, 'Longer Gone,' right?" the intern replies. "A clip from it is trending on TikTok. Or on my TikTok, anyway."

Teresa nods at me. "Call him. OK. Who do we have as backup if he doesn't work out?"

She's already on to the next thing, and I'm grateful, because heat is crawling up my chest and into my cheeks. Why do I feel weirdly guilty about this? It could be good for my relationship with Teresa, but what I'm experiencing right now is definitely more than a normal excited-about-work sensation. I'm already plotting the text I'll send to Charlie and imagining him writing back.

The last thing I do before leaving for the airport is duck into one of the makeshift "offices"—a corner surrounded by flimsy dividers—and text him. *Congratulations on the release! A twenty-something in the office reports she's heard of you.*

And I might have a friendly favor to ask you. It'd be for Teresa's campaign—it's UBI related. Feel free to say no, etc. etc. If you're up for it I'll give you the whole scoop.

Then I have to just . . . wait. I force myself to make sure that my laptop and various chargers are all packed up before I leave. He probably won't write back right away. He might not respond at all. Just because he said something at a dinner one time doesn't mean—

My phone's vibrating. I pick up so fast I almost drop it. "Hi."

He can definitely hear how flustered I sound. "Hi," Charlie says, amused. The warmth of his smile carries over all the miles between us, somehow. "Sorry, I started to type, and I just . . . I thought I'd call instead. Is that OK?"

"Of course. I mean, I'm the one asking you a favor."

"I honestly can't imagine what it is."

I thought I could keep my cool with him if I didn't have to see his perfect face, but it turns out his voice is just as bad, and my whole body is clenching. I turn to hide my smile, though I'm not sure from whom. "So I mentioned I'm working on Teresa Powell's campaign?"

"You did."

"And that she's going to announce her support for a statewide UBI pilot?"

"Mmhmm."

I sink down into my desk chair. I kick my heels off under the desk, wishing I had already changed into leggings and sneakers for the plane.

"We're holding a press conference afterward, with a handful of people speaking in support of the program. And I was wondering if you might consider being one of those people."

There's a pause. I brace for a no. "Wow. Are you sure you want . . . me?"

I automatically flip into persuasion mode. "Of course we do. You're smart, you're charming, and you have a personal connection. I think it also helps that you're unexpected. UBI sounds kind of boring to a lot of people. Having you talk about it makes it a little"—I realize too late what I'm about to say—"sexier."

All this nets me is another "Mmhmm" from him.

"*Mmhmm* what?"

"Nothing."

"Bullshit."

I'm worried that I've been too harsh until I hear a muffled laugh on the other end of the phone. "OK, yes, that was bullshit," he says. "I guess what I'm thinking is . . . are you sure you want me, *specifically*? Couldn't anyone with a recognizable name do this for you?"

I spin slowly in my chair, stockinged feet pressing against the carpet. Of course my standard pump-up speech won't work on him. So many people—especially men—hear *you're special* and don't ask any follow-up questions. But Charlie isn't that easy.

Which, of course, just makes him hotter. "I won't lie to you," I tell him. "Initially this was about asking a celebrity, generally, before it was about asking you, specifically. But I do think you, in particular, would be good at this. And I think—if you'll let me be a little obnoxious—it could be good for you. Using your voice more, this time around."

"I did say I wanted that, didn't I. And it's not obnoxious—it's the type of advice I tried to convince you to let me pay you for."

Another long pause. I'm about to step in to fill it when he sighs and says, "Is it stupid if I'm scared?" His voice sounds smaller than I thought it could, and I hunch forward, as if I'm protecting our conversation with my body. Charlie has guarded his privacy— and his sanity—so carefully for the last ten years. I should have known better than to spring something like this on him.

"Not at all. There's a reason a lot of people won't talk politics in public."

I've been trying not to think about it, but finally, I let myself imagine Charlie right now. Is he at home, barefoot in sweatpants? At an office somewhere, grabbing five minutes between meetings with label execs? I know that wherever he is, his hands are busy: fingertips drumming on his thigh or fiddling with his watch. Full of the energy that makes him so magnetic and compelling.

I could give him so many better uses for them.

"The thing is, everyone says yes to celebrities," Charlie says. "Everyone tells us our opinions are important and our ideas are good. I feel like I already take up so much space in the world. And part of me still wonders . . . do I need to take up even more?"

I'm still startled by the intimacy of his confession. How close I feel to someone I barely know. I've considered this question a thousand times. Why I or anyone else in DC should have as much power as we do over other people's lives. "You could look at it this way," I offer. "You already take up all of that space. In a lot of people's minds, anyway. This is just . . . doing something different with it. But it's entirely up to you. You don't owe this to anyone."

"Mmmm." He sounds amused again, like there's a joke he's about to let me in on. "I mean, realistically, I have to say yes though. Because if I do, then you owe me a favor, don't you?"

Wow, does this feel like flirting. Is he flirting? "Only fair," I respond.

I'm unclear if this is just him being chummy, but my skin still ripples with a shiver at the thought that it's something else.

"If I have to speak, I'm definitely going to need help writing the remarks. It turns out you don't really absorb a lot of English class when you're touring for half of high school."

Is this a yes? "Of course," I reassure him, nodding much too emphatically for a phone call. "I'm flying to LA tonight, but I'll be back Monday, and we could set up a time to go over talking points when you're ready—by phone or in person. Up to you."

"LA, huh?"

"For a friend's wedding." I'm resting my elbows on the desk now, as if he's across the table from me. As if I can get close enough to breathe him in again: that spicy, woodsy scent.

"So, thing is, I leave for Japan on Monday morning."

"I can probably sneak away for an hour for a call tomorrow? Are you on East Coast time, or . . . ?"

"As it happens," he says. "I'm in LA right now. So if you can find an hour for me in person, we can have a second drink."

VI

My jaw cracks with a yawn, and Kate's sister, Jane, gives me a polite but firm elbow to the side. "We haven't even gotten to the toasts yet," she murmurs.

"It's ten p.m. in DC," I say, but so quietly that I know she can't hear me. Jane is the maid of honor, and she takes her duties incredibly seriously. Which I do appreciate; I want Kate to have a perfect weekend. But also, I never sleep well on planes, and all my afternoon hotel nap did was make my jet-lag-induced disorientation worse. Arranging to meet Charlie after the rehearsal dinner may have been a tactical error, but it was the only time both of us were free.

Luckily, Kate's best friend from college is on my other side. "You want me to see if I can snag a coffee for you?" Pritti asks. "I need a refill anyway."

"That would be amazing, thank you." I've abused caffeine so seriously for so long that it would take a lot to keep me up past my bedtime, which is both a pro and a con of a life spent working on a politician's schedule.

I've barely seen Kate all night—par for the course—but as soon as Pritti gets up, she spots the empty chair next to me and drops into it with a sigh. "Oh my god, it feels so good to sit."

Her look is pure, uncut Kate: a perfect vintage '60s minidress—patterned, because she finds solids boring—and the kind of sky-high heels that give me a headache just from looking at them. There are rhinestone hearts on her nails because my girl has never been anything less than a maximalist.

Kate and I met our freshman year of high school, but we didn't truly bond until we discovered our mutual love of Mischief as sophomores. She's a born cheerleader who had always felt out of place at our uptight, too-cool private high school; my tendency toward bossiness wasn't winning me many friends either. But it turned out we were perfectly matched. She has the kind of enthusiasm and vision that inspire people; I have the detail orientation and pain-in-the-ass-ness required to get them to actually follow through. In a sense, Kate was my first candidate, and I've been campaigning for her ever since.

"Have you eaten anything yet?" I reach for a bread basket.

"I managed like half of the salad before my great-uncle Randolph made me listen to a lecture about *his* wedding day."

I nudge my plate in her direction. "I'm getting drinks after this. Eat. I'm sure I can get fries at the bar or something."

"You're getting drinks? *After* this?" Kate doesn't pause before helping herself to a bite of my sea bass. "God, this is good."

I haven't told Kate about the Charlie of it all yet. Not right away, when I didn't want her excitedness to rub off on me—I knew it would hamper whatever ability I could muster to act rationally. Then I thought the moment had passed and she'd be pissed at me for not telling her sooner.

Now definitely isn't the time either, so I try to change the subject. "You know how to pick a spot." And she does: we're sitting on the patio of a restaurant nestled downtown, right next to the central library. Skyscrapers soar overhead, but we're lit by the glow of paper lanterns. A fountain in the middle of the space burbles happily.

Kate won't be distracted though. "Drinks with who?"

Kate is already scanning the room, looking for whoever she needs to glad-hand next, and I know I can't drop a bomb like this.

"It's a work thing."

Which is, of course, true. But I'm still a liar.

I'll tell her after the wedding, when she's on her honeymoon and supremely relaxed. She might even be impressed that I could be so tight-lipped. Maybe I'll get Charlie to autograph a napkin tonight or something, to send her as a souvenir.

Kate leaves it, which probably says something unflattering about how much work I do. "Boring," she says and flashes me her teeth to check for any lodged parsley.

Pritti returns with a glass of wine for her and a dainty little espresso for me. "You can keep sitting," she tells Kate, but Kate is already on her feet.

"Nah, I've got to rescue Leah from her mom. Angie has gotten obsessed with the idea that her dog should be the ring bearer, which is just . . . anyway. Maya, I hope whoever you're having professional drinks with at nine p.m. on a Saturday is ready for that dress." She kisses the top of my head and goes to extricate her fiancée from a very animated conversation with her mother.

I will admit that when I picked out this dress, I had thought that, if someone at the wedding caught my eye, it might help me catch theirs back. The front V is cut low enough to show some serious skin, and my back is almost entirely bare. The skirt bells

out into a tulip shape—a ladylike nod, but it's definitely the kind
of thing I could never get away with in DC.

Two hours later, the only thing I'm thinking about is why I chose
to wear these shoes. I'm usually pretty good at enduring heels, but
it's been a day, and I shift from one foot to another, rolling out
each ankle in turn, as I stand at my hotel's bar, waiting for Charlie.

Then: a hand, warm and heavy, on my arm. Those calluses.

Charlie.

"Maya," he says.

I turn around and take him in. His cream-colored henley is
open at the throat, and a thick gold watch is strapped casually
around his wrist. He runs his fingers through his hair and all of
a sudden, I'm wide awake. The first time that I saw him, we were
both on our best behavior, trying very hard to present our most
buttoned-up selves. But now it's late, and he looks rumpled in a
way that suggests he's packed a lot into the last twelve hours too.
I feel every inch of my exposed skin under his gaze.

"Did you really get in this afternoon? You look . . ." Charlie's
eyes linger on my body, and I feel the tug of my traitorous nipples.
"I mean," he says. "You don't look like you just got off a plane."

I know I should be the one to look away, break the moment,
but I can't. Our eyes are locked, and it's like neither of us can do
anything about it. "I came straight from the rehearsal dinner, so
I had to be presentable."

The corner of Charlie's mouth pulls up into a smirk. "Presentable is one word."

My fingertips are stroking along the line of my collarbone, and I don't know how they got there. His eyes track the movement, and I wonder if it's possible that he feels as undone by this interaction as I do.

He taps the marble bar. "Have you ordered yet?"

"Haven't been able to get anyone's attention."

It takes about two seconds for Charlie to flag one of the women who've been ignoring me for the last ten minutes.

He cocks his head at me to go first, and I angle myself toward him. "A glass of white wine. Something dry." A rule someone had to teach me after I got tipsy on one too many vodka sodas as a dumbass college intern: at work drinks, always drink white wine. It's easy to sip carefully enough to stay sober, and it doesn't stain your tongue, your teeth, or your blazer when someone inevitably bumps into you.

Charlie comes from a different world than I do. He orders an old-fashioned, like he did at Denizen.

"Sounds good," the bartender says. "Just so you know," she adds, like she's telling Charlie a secret, "we're about to announce last call. You're welcome to take your drinks out there, but this area closes in fifteen minutes."

I glance backward at the lobby. The wedding party is staying at a very cute boutique hotel with low leather couches that look more suited to lounging than having a serious conversation. And it's so . . . exposed.

Panic must be visible on my face. "Tell me if I'm being presumptuous," Charlie says. "But do you want to do this in your room? You can change if you want. I'll bring up the drinks. We can order takeout or something if you're hungry. I know you're already going out of your way for this—you can at least be comfortable."

Under any other circumstances, I would say "absolutely not" to that idea. Being a young woman in politics means learning the meaning of *professional* early, digging your heels in, saying "no thank you" again and again. It's inappropriate on about thirty different levels to do this prep next to a bed. In a private room, with a closed door. And most especially with a man I was undressing with my eyes not five minutes ago. If anyone needs to avoid even a whiff of impropriety right now, it's definitely me.

But I trust Charlie. The tone of his proposal was practical and polite, not even the tiniest bit suggestive, for better or worse. And given our respective public profiles, behind a closed door might actually be our best option. Also, it just sounds *so fucking nice*. I could actually take off my shoes.

I nod. He nods back.

I glance over and see the bartender adding the orange garnish to Charlie's drink. This time, I manage to catch her eye. "Sorry, can I get a Michter's bourbon, rocks, instead?" If Charlie's drinking whiskey, I can drink whiskey.

The left corner of Charlie's mouth turns up. "Text me your room number, I'll meet you up there."

Which is how I end up sitting across from Charlie Blake in a hotel room. There are chairs over by the window, so we commandeer them for our makeshift workspace. I'm wearing my nicest leggings and an oversized cotton sweater. I have my whiskey, and he has his. My laptop is on my thighs radiating heat. That's why I'm warm, I tell myself.

"OK, so the first question we're going to have to answer

in this speech is, Why do you care about this?" My eyes catch on the way Charlie's fingers look, drumming absently against his thigh. I've spent too much time in hotel rooms to find them sexy anymore, or so I thought. "Why does it matter to a rich celebrity what happens to poor people in this country?"

Charlie nods to himself. I prepare for him to launch into a well-rehearsed monologue: the series of sound bites that he's been retelling (and I've been rereading) in glossy publications for well over a decade now.

"I . . . used to be poor people. We were middle class, but then my dad was in an accident and couldn't work anymore when I was nine. All of a sudden, we couldn't pay our bills. And I just remember looking at my parents—my mom, who worked, and my dad, who was doing everything he could to help out in other ways. Who *had* worked, up until he physically couldn't anymore. And being like, *This isn't our fault. Why won't anyone help us?*"

To see the heartbreak that crosses his face when he remembers those days—I feel callous for thinking of this like a stump speech. His dad died when Charlie was in his early twenties. These aren't talking points to him. They're his life.

That's where the best material comes from, the work part of my brain acknowledges. The rest of me wants to climb into his lap and give him a hug.

"I've gone from being poor to being rich, but that was only luck," Charlie continues. "And I don't think you should have to be lucky to have a roof over your head and three meals a day. I'm clearly not an expert, but it's not hard to wrap your head around these studies. If the data shows giving people money is the best way to help them . . . it just feels like, how can we not be giving it a shot? It makes sense to me."

"That's—you're really good at this." It takes me a few seconds to compose myself. "I'm not even sure you need me."

"Thank you." He looks bashful at my compliment. "I mean, I've told that story before, obviously."

"Yeah, but you still—I could feel it."

"You could feel it," Charlie repeats. "I like that. To hear that."

He leans back in his chair, and my eyes travel helplessly up the long, lean lines of him. The softness of his shirt, and the way it emphasizes his waist where it's tucked into his pants.

"Tell me if I'm taking us too far off track, but how did you end up in politics?" he asks. "You, you don't seem nearly cynical enough."

"You're catching me in my earnest era."

He smiles at my little joke, but it's not a real answer, and we both know it.

I could just leave it there. Redirect us to the task at hand. But Charlie is opening up for me. It's good for me—for this work we're doing, I tell myself—if I return the honesty.

The whiskey helps me tell the truth. "I thought about quitting. After my divorce. It all seemed so stupid, and fake, and pointless. Cooper, my ex, he wrecked my life, and he broke my heart. And because he did it the morning of the Iowa caucuses, it took like a month before I had any thought other than *What does this mean for the poll numbers?*"

I stretch my legs out, and I'm conscious that our thighs are now only a few inches apart. It's not possible that I feel the warmth of his skin through his pants—his unreasonably cute green chinos that are reading as way sexier than chinos have any right to be—but my body is convinced otherwise.

"But then I couldn't bring myself to go through with it," I confess. "In part because . . . honestly, I've never really *wanted* to do anything else."

Politics can be a nightmare and a drag, but it's also addictive. The high of finding the right argument, deploying the right line. Crafting a strategy that can withstand attacks from all sides. It makes you feel powerful.

But then, that's the thing. That power. How easy it is to love. How hard it is to use responsibly.

I try to choose my next words extra-carefully. "I decided that, if I was going to stay, I had to change the way I approached it. Cooper's family has been in politics for a long time, and to them, it's kind of a game. More palace intrigue than public service. I'd gotten sucked into their world and realized I'd started caring more about getting my guy on the throne, and what that would do for me, than what he would do for everyone else once he was on it. But then . . . and listen, this is so earnest."

"I'm a pop singer," he says. "I can handle earnest."

"Those years were a crash course in how power functions— one that made me want to focus on something that would give people power over their own lives. UBI feels like a North Star in that sense."

"Thank you. For telling me that." Charlie twists his watch on his wrist and is silent for a beat. "I'd heard about the divorce. Even . . . even, you know, before I read the profile."

I'm not surprised. Cooper's family has a political pedigree

to rival the Kennedys. People have cared about him since before he did anything worth caring about. And fucking a campaign intern on a senator's desk is a decent way to make headlines no matter who you are.

I shrug, like I assumed as much. "How could you not have? Cooper has always known how to make himself the center of attention."

Charlie laughs, but then his face flips to serious again. "God, it must have sucked."

There's no way to put into words how awful that whole experience was, and I'm grateful not to have to try. "Yeah. It sucked."

"Can I ask . . . you're here for a wedding? Will that be hard for you?"

I take my last gulp of whiskey. This conversation has blown past professional, and I can't bring myself to care. "Kind of? I was never a big wedding girl, so that helps. Like, when I married Cooper, it was *not* the best day of my life."

We had the ceremony at his parents' house on the Cape; it was an unseasonably warm spring day, and everyone and everything was sticky. Coop's frat-boy brother got way too drunk and picked a fight with his girlfriend, who was already mad that he hadn't proposed yet, and she spent the night crying on various shoulders. I just tried to hang on and survive it.

"And this time, I get to just be there to support Kate—my friend." I take a deep breath. "But also . . . of course it's hard. And people will be watching me, trying to gauge how hard. I sort of wish I had a date." I correct myself. "The right date. There are plenty of wrong ones available."

This time, Charlie doesn't laugh at my joke. "You didn't bring anyone?"

I look around the room. "Do you see anyone?" I offer a weary smirk. "I was going to bring my friend Gabe, who's also on the campaign, but when he had to drop out at the last minute for work stuff, it just felt easier to go it alone. My life's busy. And dating is . . . I just feel so *under a microscope*. Like, before we'd ever met, you knew way too much about me."

"Yeah," he says wryly. "And you had a picture of me in your locker."

I gasp, and then laugh at myself. There's no point denying it. "I will only admit that I did read a lot of *Teen Bop*."

Charlie folds his hands in his lap. "I do have to tell you . . . those teen magazines made a lot of shit up."

I clasp my palms against my heart in mock distress. "No!"

"They did. I'm so sorry. I don't know how to tell you this, but I was not, in fact, 'just looking for a nice girl who would get along with my mom.'"

"Nooo! What a shocking reveal!" Now we're both tipsy, and laughing, and it's hard to remember why we're here. Why I shouldn't reach out and touch his arm, just lightly, just once. To signal to him that he could touch me back, if he wanted to.

"Honestly," Charlie says, "it's nice to talk to someone who gets it."

My left thumb goes automatically to my ring finger, where I used to toy with the wedding band that isn't there. Hasn't been for over a year now. "Yeah. My husband was a piece of shit. But having an automatic plus-one . . . it's hard not to miss it."

I barely have time to chide myself for saying that out loud when Charlie says, "I could come with you."

My first instinct is to say, "You're joking," but I have just enough impulse control left to bite it back. I pause, and examine Charlie's face. There's no overhead light in here, just the desk lamps, which means he's slightly fuzzy and dim. His eyes are still so green, though, and he doesn't look like he's offering out of pity.

He looks—

"I can't," I say. "I can't ask you to do that."

—almost hopeful.

"Yeah," he says. "You could."

"Oh." I desperately wish there was just a little more whiskey left in my glass. I stare down at the melting cubes, swirling them around to hear them clink. Something to break the silence and let me stall for a second while I figure out how to respond. "Listen. We just met. And it's a big ask."

"You didn't ask. I offered," he says, not taking his eyes off me. "And anyway, it's not that big of a deal. We'll toast, we'll dance, we'll maybe do some crying. I have been known to be a wedding crier, so fair warning." He's doing his best to make it sound casual, and my mind is spinning, my pulse is racing in ways that are not at all casual. I know I have to turn him down.

Charlie is too big of a risk to take—especially for me, especially right now. If he's only offering because he feels sorry for me, it'll break my heart. And if he's offering for any other reason . . . I can't even let myself think about it.

Particularly because getting involved with a celebrity who's recently reentered the public eye is the definition of *making myself the story*.

"I really can't," I repeat.

"OK," Charlie says, eyes shifting to the hotel notepad on the desk.

My laptop screen has gone to sleep while we've been talking, and I tap the keys to bring it back to life. "So. Tell me more about your mom."

An hour later, we're wrapping up. I've kept it as professional as I can, but my mind keeps wandering to the idea of Charlie coming to the wedding. What he'd look like in a suit from up close. The way he might catch my eye across the room and grin, or put a hand on the small of my back to guide me through a crowd.

"Are you excited for Japan?" I ask as I email Gabe the notes from our conversation.

"I think so." He sees me waiting for more. "I love Japan. I'm just feeling anxious about the work part." The ice in Charlie's drink has long since melted; he tips back the rocks glass and takes a final sip.

"It seems like the single is doing really well."

"Better than I could have hoped. It's not that." Charlie chews on his lower lip, his face distracted. "It's been a while since I was inside the fame machine. I barely got out alive, the first time. And it's like . . . am I really doing this to myself again? Taking all of those risks, even though I know the cost?"

"You're a lot older now."

"Hey!" he responds, trying to lighten the mood.

"And *wiser*," I amend. "Now you know the world won't end if you decide to leave again."

"If there's one thing I've learned, in my many, many long years," Charlie says. "It's that the world rarely ends when you think it will."

My brain flashes back to that day, waking up in an Iowa hotel room, jet lag crusting my eyes, sunshine streaming in because I forgot to shut the blinds last night. I had twenty things on my mind already, emails to send, to-do's to accomplish. This was the biggest job I'd ever taken on, and I was about to find out how I was doing at it. I thought—I hoped—I might be doing really well.

Then I saw what was on my phone.

Fuck it, I think. I've already survived one end of the world. Don't I get to have a little fun in the afterlife?

"Come to the wedding with me." I brace against my own impulsiveness. This is a bad idea. I *know* it's a bad idea. But I want to give myself something I want, just because I want it.

No one will ever have to know, I reason. Kate and Leah are having a phone-free wedding, which struck me as almost absurdly Hollywood of them, but which, to be fair, I am also very much looking forward to. A rare opportunity for me to totally unplug from work. And the added benefit of no Instagram record.

And I couldn't get Kate a better present than bringing Charlie Blake to her wedding. Even if she is going to lose her shit when I spring this on her tomorrow.

"Are you sure?" he asks.

"Unless you've rescinded your offer."

"I was actually trying to decide if I should make one more plea before I left."

"You really like weddings, huh?"

"Sure," he says. "That's what I like."

My heart starts to thrum dangerously in my chest, so I narrow my eyes. "What, are you a great dancer or something?"

He laughs. "Maya, you of all people have seen my moves."

I have, technically. Mischief was trying to compete with NSYNC and Backstreet Boys when they first started out, and they did some of that cheesy choreographed stuff. But they abandoned it pretty quickly, and that was one of the things I always loved about them. They weren't pageant boys. The way they moved on stage—it was goofy sometimes, and silly. But you could tell the music was part of them, the same way it was part of me.

"Oh god," I blurt out, the reality of what bringing him would mean settling in. "It's very possible that you're gonna hear a Mischief song at this thing. When I said I met Kate when I was fourteen . . . I met her because we co-ran Making Mischief."

He doesn't miss a beat. "Oh, then I have to thank her in person. Tell her about how much I liked the shirts."

"She's going to lose it."

"Honestly, it'll be good for my ego. No one's flipped out about me in a long time."

"Oh, did you *want* me to recite my *Tiger Beat* factoids? Because I probably still remember a choice quote or two . . ."

"No," he says, holding up his hands to stop me. "Please don't. But just so you know, I do like dancing. I'm not very good at it. But I like it."

"Same." I'm clasping my hands together in my lap to keep from touching him. "Cooper hated dancing. He would do one verse of a slow song for a photo. I was always alone out there."

Charlie smiles at me so tenderly. Something inside of me loosens. "I promise you, Maya," he says, and his voice is gentle. Almost coaxing. "I'm not doing anything for a photo."

I can't help myself; I hold his eye contact. The moment between us attenuates, stretches. Becomes . . . whatever it's going to become. But I've already tested my limits tonight, so I force myself to be the first to look away.

He shakes his head. "All right, time for me to go." He stands and walks across the room, opening the door so that he's haloed by the bright hallway light. "Get some sleep. We have big boogie plans for tomorrow."

"*Big boogie plans?*" I repeat as I go to meet him.

"I have a way with words. I'm a pop star, remember?" There's a pause, and I think we're both mulling over whether we should . . . hug? We did just have a pretty personal conversation. And he's going to be my date to my best friend's wedding tomorrow.

But I know myself. And I know that if I start touching him, I won't be able to stop. I nudge the door, and Charlie shoves his hands in his pockets.

"Good night," I say.

Charlie nods. "Good night."

I watch him walk down the hall with long, confident strides and wonder what exactly I just got myself into.

VII

The first thing I have to do this morning is strategize how to reveal to Kate that I invited Charlie Blake to her wedding. Decades of friendship have taught me that carbs are the easiest way to soften her up, and I show up at the venue at 9:00 a.m. sharp, a double-toasted bagel with lox and extra cream cheese in my bag.

"Maya!" Kate reaches for a hug when she sees me, but she's restrained by the woman who's arranging her wild mass of hair. I lean in to brush a kiss against her cheek. "You're not due until ten thirty."

"I have a surprise for you. Well, two surprises." I pull the bagel out of my bag, and predictably, Kate's wide hazel eyes light up.

"Oh, thank god," she says. "I was too nervous to eat before, and I had two cups of coffee."

The hairstylist adds one last bobby pin and steps back with a flourish. "Eat that, and then we can get going on your makeup," she says. "I'll tell Thalia you're ready for her in ten?"

Kate takes a gleeful bite of bagel. Her energy is *so* different than mine was on my wedding day. So happy. Excited. "What's the other surprise?" she asks around a mouthful.

The venue is a beautiful old Hollywood mansion, high on a

hill in Silver Lake. We're in what must once have been a drawing room, with thick carpet on the floors and imposing leather chairs gathered around a fireplace. Kate's chair is angled toward a floor-to-ceiling window so that her face is bathed in natural light, making her look even softer, younger.

I lean against the frame. "The business meeting I had last night."

"I'm nervous about where this is going." She leans forward, breakfast momentarily forgotten.

"I swear to god it was about work. But it was also with Charlie Blake."

Kate examines my face carefully. "You're not kidding."

"I'm not kidding."

Kate is an adult woman. She's been working in the film industry doing PR since college, and her fiancée is a well-known celebrity stylist. She's met more than her share of famous people. But right now, she looks like a teenage girl. Her face is bright with wonder. "What does that have to do with me?"

"He's coming to the wedding. As my date."

"Maya. McPherson. WHAT!"

"I don't know!! Is your cousin's plus-one still open? Your great-aunt Sophie didn't make the trip, right?"

As soon as Kate starts laughing, so do I. This is the kind of situation we might have dreamed up when we were experimenting with fanfic—absurd fantasy wish fulfillment And yet. Somehow it's real.

"As if I wouldn't find a seat for Charlie fucking Blake! But yes, my cousin Blaine went nuclear with his ex's dirty laundry on TikTok, so that spot's very open. Wait, OK, start at the beginning.

How did this *happen*?" Kate asks, pausing to breathe. She's gripping my arm so hard it's going to leave a mark.

"He saw the *Vogue* profile. He wanted to talk to me about consulting on his comeback strategy."

"Oh my god," she says, her eyes slits. "You told him no, didn't you. You said no to *Charlie Blake*. And he, what? Chased you to LA to convince you to say yes? Have you swooned in his arms yet? Is he going to propose?"

"Oh my god, none of that!" I know I have the dumbest grin on my face, but I can't stop myself. It's like we're back in her teen bedroom, splayed on the floor with CD booklets around us. "I mean, you're right, I did say no to the consulting. But then I asked him to do a campaign thing for Teresa, and we had to talk about his speech, and we were both in LA, and then we started talking about weddings. And it just . . . happened."

"*It just happened.* You are completely ridiculous."

I throw up my hands. "It did, though! This whole thing is as much a mystery to me as it is to you."

"Oh, I don't know about a *mystery*." Kate settles back in her chair and picks up the bagel she abandoned right around the moment Charlie's name first came out of my mouth. She looks at me again, more carefully this time. "You like him." It's not a question.

"I have liked him since you've known me! Of course I fucking like him."

"No," Kate says, with exaggerated patience. "I mean, you *like* him."

I resist the urge to cover my face. Trust Kate to verbalize exactly what I've been trying not to think ever since that first dinner. I give her the same talk I've been giving myself. "He's charming. And smart. But I barely know him."

"OK, OK." Kate is sneaky: she seems so chill that I sometimes forget she's a little snake. "And? Do you like him?"

I fold. "Fuck me. You know I do."

"Maya, that's a good thing!"

"Is it?"

"Why wouldn't it be?"

"Well, for instance," I start ticking things off on my fingers. "I *have* had a crush on him since I was fourteen. Which means I'm in way too deep. *And* he's famous. Which is the absolute last thing I need in my life right now. I *just* made a promise to Teresa that I would not land my name in the news again during her campaign." God, I can't even think about the headlines that the combination of our names would inspire. I've been feeling warm and open—talking with Kate, joking around, like this is possible—but just saying those words brings me back down to earth again.

If nothing else, Cooper should have taught me never to trust a man with easy charm again. But also, Charlie is just not possible. Not for me. Not now, and probably not ever.

"Anyway," I say, trying to put the walls back up. "I mean, no offense to me, but he dates literal models. I don't think he's interested in me that way."

Kate rolls her eyes. "Men don't come to weddings with women they're indifferent about."

"I was complaining about feeling lonely last night. And he likes to dance." OK, when I say that out loud, it sounds a little . . . weak.

Kate decides to give me a break. "I'm glad you have a date," she says. "I know it's complicated, being here. And I appreciate it."

"It's not—"

"It is," she says. "It's OK."

I shrug. She's right, and also, I think it's less difficult than I expected. So far, anyway. "My wedding felt like an obligation," I tell her. "Yours feels like a celebration."

Kate came out when we were freshmen in college. A few years later, California passed Proposition 8, which banned gay marriage in the state. I might not have dreamed of a white wedding, but Kate always had, and it crushed her to know that so many people were committed to making sure she didn't get one.

And the truth is, I got married because I thought it was next up on the adulthood checklist. Cooper couldn't have been more suitable. It was, I thought, "the right move."

Kate is getting married because she's in love.

I feel tears threatening and beat them back. I am going to cry—it's inevitable—but not before the ceremony even starts. "It's easy to be happy for you," I tell her.

"Maya!" Kate bats at her eyes, and of course that's when the makeup artist comes to retrieve her and tsk-tsks us for making our eyes puffy.

After that, the hours pass in a blur, and the next thing I know, I'm standing next to twenty-three-year-old Danny, his arm linked through mine. Kate's six-year-old niece, Sabrina, is up ahead of us, scattering rose petals; Kate herself is just around the corner, about to be revealed. A string quartet plays, and as I hear our cue, Danny and I take our first step onto the worn stone path.

I flash back to five years ago: instead of Danny's arm slung through mine, it's my father's. The air was briny, and my heart thrummed in my chest. I had wanted to wear the veil because I thought it would look romantic, and in photos, it did. But walking toward Cooper, the world was blurry and faraway, and I thought, *Shouldn't I be able to see my future more clearly?*

Now there's nothing to block my vision of Charlie in his seat, turning toward me. And the way he looks when he does. His eyes are warm and soft. Enveloping.

He's wearing a perfectly tailored suit, his hair and his eyes shining against the crisp black and white of his outfit. That gold watch is back on his wrist, heavy and thick. He doesn't look like the boy I yearned for at all, I think. And somehow I want him more.

"Wow," he mouths as we walk past. And despite everything I said to Kate this morning, he looks like he means it. My stomach twists, and I tighten my grip on Danny's arm.

I smile back, lingering on him at least two beats too long.

Kate did us a favor with the bridesmaid's dresses. Since it's just me and Jane, she told us to find something light colored that we would wear again. I took a trip into New York with the intention of scouring all the good vintage stores and ended up buying the first dress I tried on: a champagne silk number with thin straps holding up a simple straight neckline and a drop waist that oozes 1920s glamour. I thought about going over the top with jewelry but settled on a pair of sapphire studs with simple enamel detailing and a minimalist gold bracelet around my left wrist. The hair stylist pulled mine back in a sleek low bun, so there's no hiding my face behind it. With Charlie's eyes on me, I feel bare in the best way possible.

We all stand under the chuppah, late afternoon light filtering around us. I clutch my bouquet to my chest, and I'm overwhelmed by the sweet scent of lilies and how hard my heart is beating. How happy I feel.

I make it to the vows before the tears threaten again. "The thing about you, Kate, is that you're very easy to love," Leah says. "You've got this big smile and tons of enthusiasm. You're a walking ray of sunshine. Imagine how much that pissed me off when I first met you.

"But then, when you asked me out at that after-party, that's when I learned that you are gutsy. You are fierce. You go after what you want. I couldn't believe that what you wanted was cynical, curmudgeonly me. I'm a little bit harder to love." She holds up her hands to Kate, who's already starting to protest. "No, no, it's true. And it's OK. For a long time, I wondered when you were going to get sick of me. Go find someone who is as bold and bright as you are."

Kate laughs through mounting tears and mouths, "Never." I try to stifle a sniffle and fail.

"And then you said you wanted to love me for the rest of your life. And you said it enough times that I realized that it didn't matter if I understood why. You knew exactly who you were getting, and you always wanted more. You had chosen me. And I had to start choosing me too. So, Kate, I promise that I will try to love myself the way you love me. And I will try to be worthy of the gift of your love, and your confidence, and your light, and your warmth, every day of our lives."

I can barely see the guests through my tears. But when I catch a glimpse of Charlie, he's wiping the corners of his eyes too.

"I need a drink," Danny announces as soon as we make our way back into the building. "I bet there's not even a line at the bar yet." He doesn't wait for my response, just bounds away like a puppy. Was I ever *that* young?

I feel the brush of a hand graze the small of my back and hear someone say, "Hey."

I spin around to see Charlie beaming at me. The effect of him in that suit is even more overwhelming up close. A few years ago, a paparazzi caught him coming out of the gym, shirtless, on a summer afternoon. I felt a little guilty looking at the images, knowing they were invasive, but they're seared into my mind anyway, and I can picture his skin under his clothes with painful accuracy. The corded muscles of his arms and the broadness of his chest. The fuzz of hair in the center of his sternum, dipping down below his navel. He looks so civilized right now, but my thoughts are not.

Charlie takes another step toward me. He's close enough to touch me, but he doesn't. "You make an outstanding bridesmaid."

"Thank you." I meet his gaze for a second, and then lose my courage and look down again just as quickly. I'm not sure how to interact with him. We've always had the pretext of work before. Now we're just . . . us.

"I told you I'd cry."

That does the trick. I laugh. "I mean, I wept! Oh god—how fucked is my mascara? Don't say it's fine. I know it's not. You have to be honest with me. That's like, your number-one responsibility as a date."

"I thought that was the dancing," Charlie says, but he's already reaching out to cup his palm to my chin, turning my face so that he can see better. His skin is so warm against mine, and there are those calluses again, a prickle against my cheek. Charlie examines me seriously, and I try to remember how to breathe. "It kind of looks intentional," he says after a minute. "Like a smoky eye thing, maybe?"

My shoulders shake with a laugh. "That bad, huh?"

"I'm sorry." He hangs his head in mock shame.

We get in line for the bar together, and I wipe delicately at my under eyes, trying to do whatever damage control I can. I survey the room to see if I can spot Kate—I want to introduce them sooner rather than later—but she's nowhere to be found. I hope that means she and Leah are hiding out for a few minutes together.

Then paranoia of being in public starts to tug at the hem of my dress, like a little kid who's been ignored at a party for too long. *You've been having a nice time*, it says. *You've let your guard down. What did you miss while you were flirting with Charlie just now?*

My skin crawls, and I can't tell if it's because I'm actually being watched or because this has become my body's natural reaction to being out in the world. I try not to make a big deal about glancing around the room, looking to see if anyone is noticing me. Or, god forbid, noticing that Charlie and I are here together.

But even with my fear-goggles on, I can't make myself believe that anyone cares. Kate and I are still friendly with some of the girls from the Making Mischief days, but not close enough for any of them to be here. And it's not like he's the only celebrity on hand. Kate's colleagues from Sony are milling about, more than a few of them with models and actresses as their plus-ones, and the wedding is sprinkled with Leah's styling clients—ultracool girls like Ayo Edebiri and Jenny Slate.

As Charlie hands me a G&T, I order myself to relax. "Want to do a loop?" I ask. "The grounds here are supposed to be beautiful."

Charlie gestures. "You lead the way."

We pass by a rectangular swimming pool and walk from there into the gardens. I trail my fingertips across flower petals and tilt my head up, enjoying the golden hour.

"God, I love spring," Charlie says. "Especially in LA—the jasmine."

"It's one of my favorites. My mom didn't let me wear perfume when I was in middle school, so I used to pick it off of bushes and rub it on my wrists before I went out." The scent always brings me back to the heady rush of early adolescence. How it felt to try to get away with something for the first time. I was so bold back then. I only ever looked forward, at what I wanted.

"Did it work?"

I look at him quizzically.

"The perfume hack?"

"It faded pretty quickly. But the first boy I ever kissed told me I smelled good, so I'm counting that as a win."

"First kiss!" Charlie says. "Tell me more."

"We were thirteen, and we were at an arcade. He was sweaty

from playing *DDR—Dance Dance Revolution*." Charlie laughs, open and bright. "Anyway, what about you? I know what *Tiger Beat* said, but who was your actual first kiss?"

"That one they got right. Sarah Kendrick. We were nine. Recess."

I know it's stupid, but I'm jealous of her.

"But OK," Charlie says. He's steered us toward a little gazebo, and he sits on the wrought-iron bench at its center. When I slide next to him, I'm exquisitely aware of how close we are. "What was your first *real* kiss? Like the first time—you know. You felt it."

I don't have to ask him what he means by *it*. It's basically what I'm feeling right now: an ache between my hip bones. A lump in my throat, but the good kind. My skin tingling with excitement.

"That didn't happen until I was sixteen. I remember saying to a friend afterward, 'I understand why we kiss with tongues now.'" I'm glad Charlie and I are sitting side by side, so that he can't see the flush on my face. It's equal parts the memory and describing it to him. Thinking about how turned on I was then . . . and how turned on I am now. "The guy was a mess, but he knew what he was doing. We only hooked up for a few weeks, but I felt drunk the entire time."

"Yeah?"

Am I imagining that Charlie's voice is a little bit lower—rougher—than it was a few seconds ago?

The next words fall out of my mouth before I can stop them. "I miss that. Feeling that way about someone."

"Yeah," Charlie says again. I can hear his breathing getting slow and shallow.

We look out over the dusky haze of Los Angeles together. We're still not touching. I feel how much we're not touching. I am both desperate and terrified to find out what happens next.

Then I hear my name being called by a giddy Kate.

"Maya!" she says. "Maya! Jane said she saw you walking over here, and—"

I'm up and down the steps of the gazebo, Charlie just behind me. Kate stops short when she sees us.

"Oh," she says. "Hi. I didn't mean to interrupt."

"Not at all," Charlie says. "Congratulations. What a moving ceremony."

"Kate," I say, unnecessarily. "This is Charlie. Charlie, Kate."

"Nice to meet you," Kate says. "Sorry, this day has been very surreal, so I can't really . . . process this properly." Her careful hairdo is already coming undone, and I like it this way. She looks more like herself.

"Maya and I were just admiring the view," Charlie says, motioning back toward the gazebo. "Want to join us?"

"I would love," Kate says, "to admire the view."

Charlie moves aside, extending his arm for us to go first, and Kate and I settle ourselves on the bench. He leans against one of the wooden railings, and I'm forcibly reminded of Angela Chase's immortal line: "He leans great." Charlie, of course, does.

The sun is slipping below the horizon, turning the sky rose and cornflower blue. Kate leans her head on my shoulder, and I press a kiss into her hair. I let myself take in how Charlie looks in profile, framed in the very last of the daylight: his golden hair burnished and his eyes brighter than ever.

A few minutes ago, I was a wire pulled taut by his presence. I thought Kate puncturing the moment would feel deflating, but instead, I'm more at peace than I've been in a long time.

After a few minutes, Kate stands up. "Phew. Thanks," she says. "I didn't realize how badly I needed that."

Charlie nods. "Probably the only practical thing I learned in my misspent youth: how to take a beat at a party."

"Well, I appreciate it."

There's a pause, and then Kate just throws her arms around him, wrapping him up in an exuberant hug. I can see her realize what she's doing as she's doing it, but it's too late to stop herself, and anyway, of course Charlie hugs her back.

"It's so nice to meet you," Kate says, laughing, as they separate. "And so weird."

"Nice to meet you too," Charlie says.

"I have to get back," Kate says. "But I'll see you guys soon."

Charlie turns to me. "Do you want to go?" he asks. "Do you want a jacket? Or another drink?"

I should say yes to all of those things. But I shake my head. Because what I would like more is to stay suspended in the delicate soap bubble of a world that's just Charlie and me, and no one else. To ask how many parties he's been at where he had to escape and steal moments to himself. When he learned that, and how.

I also want to demand to know why I feel so fucking comfortable with him, whether we're talking or not. And how he knew how to charm Kate by saying nothing at all.

We start walking again farther into the garden, aimlessly, heading nowhere. "So. Do you have your set lists planned for the shows?" I ask. He's playing an album preview while he's in Tokyo.

"I do. I even added a couple of surprises."

"Surprises like . . ." I start, but Charlie just raises his brows. "OK, then, be a tease."

"OK, OK." He grins at me. "I'm planning a few covers, but there are no Mischief songs on it. Yet."

"Yet?"

"I couldn't pick one. They all sound the same to me now, honestly. I've sung them too many times, you know?"

"Well, my favorite was always 'Until It Rains.'" It's sweeping and achingly romantic. And Charlie sings lead on two of the verses. "Kate's too."

"I trust that you two have good taste." Charlie watches me, and there's a question on his face. I'm not sure that I know what it is. And even if I did, I certainly don't know my answer.

VIII

I keep expecting Charlie to wander off at some point during the party. Cooper never stuck by my side for long; he was trained early in the art of schmoozing, and he works every room he's in. But Charlie just . . . hangs out with me. Through the rest of cocktail hour, and while we eat salads and salmon and raise our glasses for toasts. We murmur jokes and make conversation with the other people at our table. He flags down a waiter when he notices that our seatmate's glass is empty.

When the music starts, he's one of the first people on the dance floor. As much as I genuinely love to dance, nerves hold me back at first. In order to dance, you have to forget to worry about whether you look stupid. And that has not been very easy lately.

Charlie doesn't care about my cold feet. "Uh-uh," he says, shaking his head. "You said you wanted to dance, and now you *will* dance."

The DJ starts with oldies, the way they always do, to give the older people their moment before they call it a night. "Twist and Shout." Colored lights are strobing all around us, but the green of Charlie's eyes is still clear and bright. He's shrugged off his jacket, but his tie is still tight at his throat.

I take his outstretched hands and let go of the thoughts wriggling through my mind. Charlie twists in close to me, and then away again, grinning like he's enjoying being a tease. It makes my stomach tighten with want. Aside from our clasped hands, he doesn't touch me. Doesn't pull me in those final, crucial inches. The air around me feels like it's electrified, like I'm surrounded by a force field that buzzes just above my skin.

Charlie's grin and his enthusiasm are contagious—and not just to me. The dance floor fills up, nudging us closer and closer together as the song ends and fades into another one. Charlie runs his hands through his hair, and I catch the scent of him again, humid and intimate. The spice of his cologne, and underneath that, the faint musk of sweat and skin. It takes every ounce of self-restraint not to press my face into the side of his neck and just inhale and inhale and inhale.

The last strains of "Ain't Too Proud to Beg" fade out, and they're replaced by the opening notes of "I'm on Fire." Kate's a big Springsteen fan, and we used to listen to this on repeat every August, when it was too hot to breathe and we were overflowing with teenage longing.

Now I let the music rub up against my thighs, my waist, where I wish Charlie was touching me. "I've got a bad desire," Bruce sings.

Charlie reaches for my hand again, but this time, he doesn't keep his distance. He reels me in and presses me close. I can't help gasping at the suddenness of it. The warmth of the whole length of his body against mine.

My hips slot against his, and his thigh nudges gently between mine, a perfect little press that shoots through every nerve. It's perfectly PG in theory, but the way my entire body is humming, it feels anything but—like I can't believe we're doing this in public. I wonder if he's as aware as I am of my nipples straining through the thin fabric of my dress. There's nothing I can do about it. There's nothing to do but give in to the way he feels against me. I go molten.

When the song ends, I look up, and our eyes lock. And I know Charlie can see it on my face. "Maya," he says, his voice rough. He sounds despairing, almost. Anguished.

The DJ's announcement cuts him off. "I believe we have a little surprise for the brides," he booms into the speakers.

Charlie steps back, and I can't help it: I panic. He saw the lust I didn't even try to hide, and it was too much, and now he's freaking out. He thought maybe this would be easy and fun, but I took it too far. And now he'll be warm but distant. He'll make an excuse to leave early. And I'll be in this beautiful dress at a perfect party, kicking myself for not managing to keep myself under control.

I watch, frozen, as Charlie goes up to the DJ booth and . . . someone hands him an acoustic guitar.

Where the fuck did he find someone with a guitar?

"Hi," he says into the microphone. "I'm Charlie. I was an, um, a last-minute addition to this beautiful wedding. Which means I didn't have time to get a gift. But I thought that, if the brides permit, I'd offer a little unscheduled entertainment." He looks in Kate's direction, and she's grinning and laughing, nodding vigorously as Leah squeezes her waist.

Charlie strums the first chord, and my body recognizes the sound before my mind does. I would know the opening to "Until

It Rains" anywhere. The music sweeps across my skin, leaving a trail of goose bumps in its wake. "I thought I knew what love was, before I met you," Charlie sings, his eyes glinting under the lights. He looks so perfectly natural like this, holding a Gibson, commanding an audience. I can't believe he lived without it for so long. "I thought I knew the seasons' change."

I'm still standing on the dance floor, and I'm rooted to the spot. Charlie meets my gaze, and I flush everywhere, from the crown of my head to the tips of my toes. His eyes on me feel like an answer to the look I gave him just a few minutes ago.

I'm standing here in the desert, the next lyric goes. This song has always had a direct line to my heart, maybe because Kate and I grew up in drought-stricken Southern California. I knew exactly what it felt like to want things—love and weather—that felt impossibly out of reach. *And I'll be loving you until it rains.*

When Mischief performed the song, they made a production out of it. It was a puppy's plea; the promise of boys for whom *forever* was still too big to mean anything real. But with just Charlie's voice, the song becomes soulful and yearning. There's a scrape as he reaches for a low note—one of Devin's—and he strains a bit for Chris's high tones. But it doesn't matter. I can feel him feel the song.

I can feel him feel it everywhere in my body.

When Charlie plays the last note, there's a moment of silence so complete it almost echoes. And then the crash and thunder of applause.

That's what finally unsticks me from my spot. I try to make it look casual as I hurry out of the room. It's just too much at once—Charlie's charm, and his smile, and the way he asked me what my favorite song was and played it. Played it like *that*. And looked at me like he meant it. I need the snap of the night air against my skin to get myself under control.

I walk out toward the garden where the pool is sitting, empty and lonely. I lean down and dip a hand in, watching ripples spread out from my palm. Something is moving through me, a feeling too big to name. All my carefully cultivated distance and self-protection dissolving, dissipating.

"Maya." Charlie saw me leave. And he's wondering why.

I try to compose myself before I stand up. When I rise, I feel the way my dress skims over my body, and exactly how nearly naked I am underneath it. I'm covered in goose bumps.

I find my voice with some effort. "You were incredible in there."

He brushes away the compliment like he barely heard it. "I know it was . . ."

Insanely sexy? Impossibly romantic? A literal dream come true?

A wry, self-deprecating smile twists at his mouth. ". . . presumptuous."

I'm truly having trouble locating words. "No, it really—it really wasn't."

"Then why did you leave? I thought you were—we were—" He reaches for me and then stops himself, his hand flexing and clenching in the empty air.

I'm still terrified of what it means to let this happen. But I can't let Charlie think he's alone in this. "We are," I say, taking a step toward him. It feels like giving in to the pull of gravity: inexorable. A relief. "I mean, I am."

"So then, just now . . ."

"It was a little overwhelming. But in a good way."

"Too much?"

He's close enough to touch, and finally, I do. I reach out a hand and curl it around his stark black lapel. Instantly I feel like a circuit has been completed, like the energy that's been coursing through me all night has found a way to ground. My rational mind is still singing its chorus: *Stop, stop, stop, stop, stop.* But I can barely hear it over my body's certainty that this is the right thing to do. "No, not too much. I mean . . . To be honest, I want more."

He looks at my hand. Looks at me. "Good," he says, deadly serious, but his eyes are shining. "Because I do too. A lot more."

And then he fits his palm around my jaw, and presses his lips to mine.

IX

Charlie kisses like he sings: sensuous and with conviction. One hand is pressed against my cheek, hot and possessive; the other is splayed across the exposed section of my back, his long fingers gently kneading my skin.

I realize my own hands are in his hair, threaded through as if I'm trying to pin him in place, and maybe I am. I force one to release, but it has a mind of its own. Now that I know I'm allowed, I have to touch the hard, flat plane of his chest where it's pressed against me, to feel the dip of his waist and the strength of his back. I keep meaning to let him go, but I pull him closer instead.

We kiss until we're both gasping for air, until I ache everywhere with wanting. I haven't made out like this since I was a teenager, fully clothed and reckless with need. His hands move to my ass, grasping for the closeness that we wouldn't let ourselves find on the dance floor, pressing me against him over and over and over again.

I don't know how long it's been when he pulls away long enough to say, "I don't want to make you miss your best friend's wedding."

I can't help laughing. He sounds so serious. I barely remember where we are, let alone what's happening around us. "She got married hours ago."

"The party, then."

"The party's fine without us."

In the inches of space between us, I can see that I've already wrecked him: his lips are tinted with my lipstick, and his hair has gone from stylishly undone to a legitimate mess. At some point I got the first three buttons of his shirt undone, and his tie hangs loosely against his collarbone. God, he looks so hot rumpled. I can't let myself look between his legs, but I know he's hard the same way he must know I'm wet—because our make out left little to the imagination. I didn't mean to let myself do this—I *didn't*.

But now that we've started, I can't bear the thought of stopping.

"I'll tell Kate we're leaving," I say, decisive. "If you call us a car."

Charlie examines me for a moment, as if I might not be telling him the whole truth. I don't know how to communicate that it's just now that I stopped keeping things from him. He must see it in my eyes, though, because after a moment, he says, simply, "Deal."

It feels impossible to step away from him, to leave the circle of heat and need we've created between our bodies. But I do. I find Kate still dancing, drunk and exhilarated. I pull her in for a hug and whisper in her ear—sharing just enough to let her know my bridesmaid duties will be relinquished. It's so loud that no one hears her when she yells, "Of course you are!! You deserve some good dick!!!!"

I quickly detour inside to grab my things, and when I reach the driveway, Charlie's standing there, back to me, hands in his pockets. I stop short and let myself look at him. He was skinny as a teenager, but he's filled out now, and I shiver involuntarily, imagining his body hovering over mine. The weight of him against me, inside of me, filling me up and turning me inside out.

I could change my mind. I'm more than halfway ruined, but there's still time to send him home. To be smart and strategic; to keep this relationship in the realm of plausible deniability. One little make out, a teenage fantasy fulfilled. A tipsy little wedding slip. Nothing more.

But then Charlie turns around and sees me, and smiles. And I know it was never really a choice.

I walk to his side, and he reaches over and takes my bag from me with one hand and grabs my hand with the other. It's such a simple touch. Reassuring. Easy. It overrides any instinct but to keep touching him.

In the back of the car, he only lets go in order to rest that palm on my thigh. It's another light touch, but this one doesn't feel as easy. I'm excruciatingly conscious of the whisper-thin layer of fabric separating his skin from mine and the torturous inches between where his hand is and where I want it.

The drive between Silver Lake and downtown isn't long, especially at this time of night, but it seems to take forever. So does the suddenly-miles-long walk across the lobby, our heads ducked, and the glacially slow elevator up to my floor. We're quiet the whole way. Like talking would break the spell of what's happening between us.

Charlie keeps a respectful distance every second we're in public, but as soon as I close the door behind us, he has me up against it. It's as cool on my back as he is hot on my front, and my brain starts cataloging the many things I somehow haven't imagined doing with Charlie. This. The infinite possibilities of my body and his.

His nimble fingers find the hidden zipper at my side immediately, and he tugs it down. The dress isn't complicated. All I have to do is shrug it off my shoulders, and in an instant, it's a puddle at my feet. I'm still wearing my heels, and for a moment, I'm another person entirely, one I haven't been in a long time: sexy and brazen and unafraid.

Charlie steps back a millimeter to look at me, breaking eye contact as his vision travels down my body. He shrugs off his suit jacket, tossing it on a nearby chair. He's working his bottom lip between his teeth, and his fingers slowly scrape the back of his neck, contemplative. I half expect him to crack his knuckles when he bends down with purpose to press kisses to each of my breasts—brief, teasing—before dropping to his knees. He presses his face against my stomach, hands on either side of my hips. I throw my head back and gasp. Then those hands slide down, further: to my thighs, my knees. My calves. I look down to see him undoing the straps of my shoes. I let out a delighted laugh.

He looks up. "What?"

I thread my hands through his hair again. His eyes are dark with a promise that I feel right to my core. "You. Of course you're good at this."

"Oh, you mean that's the one bit of trivia you didn't retain from my *Teen People* Q&A?" He slides off one heel, and then the other. "Is it cheesy that I want to make your knees buckle? You're always so composed."

I laugh. Now that my feet are on firm ground, Charlie runs

his hands up my legs again, pressing his mouth against the inside of my thighs. Heat and pressure are building right where I want him most. My fingers twitch. My own breath hitches.

"Good," he says in response to the sound. He lifts one of my legs over his shoulder and licks me, a slick, commanding slide of tongue over underwear.

My hands scrabble against the door for purchase, trying to get him where I want him and to keep my balance at the same time. His mouth finds me over and over again through the fabric, and I let out a soft, keening noise.

"Here we go." His voice is low, rough, coaxing. "Can I take these off too?"

"Yes—yes—yes please."

And now I'm naked with Charlie kneeling in front of me. He's still fully clothed, but hardly crisp, and I can't help admiring the contrast between earlier and now as he presses me back against the door, his tongue urging my legs open wider and my body complying. At a certain point, my knees *do* buckle, and we stumble into bed together.

Charlie is single-minded. He keeps his tongue hot and wet against my clit, his fingers now moving inside of me, and his other hand reaching up to pinch my nipple. I can feel the inevitable happening, waves starting to build in my body. My thighs tremble; my hands clench and unclench against the sheets. I don't know what I'm holding out against, only that I don't want this to be over, that I don't want to give up this last little bit of composure, that I'm scared that I—that this is—

But I can't hold back. And finally, my mind goes dark, and all

I can do is feel: pressure, and friction, and his tongue insistent, and his fingers probing, there, and *there*, and oh—release.

Oh, *fuck*.

When I open my eyes, Charlie is kneeling over me, his hands on either side of my head, a few strands of hair falling down in his face, and he's, looking, to be honest, a little self-satisfied.

I grin up at him, a little self-satisfied too. "You're good with your mouth."

"I'm glad to hear it."

I pull his head down toward mine, and I can taste myself on him as our lips meet. My nakedness feels indecent against the suit's fabric.

I keep my mouth pressed to his while I undo the buttons of his shirt and push it off his shoulders, reach down for his belt and then his fly. I pull him out of his briefs and pause, taking a moment to appreciate him—it's only fair after the inspection he gave me back at the door. There's that adage about big hands, big dick, but the other thing I have found to be true is beautiful hands, beautiful dick. In this, Charlie is no exception. He lets me flip us over so I can wrap my mouth around him. He groans, his hands making a welcome mess of my hair as I draw circles with my tongue.

But he doesn't let me stay long. Soon, he's pulling me up so we're at eye level, his hands cupping either side of my face. "I'm not going to last if you keep that up. I've been thinking about this longer than I'm willing to admit."

God. I don't want his confession right now, don't want to have to think about the implications. I just want to touch every inch of him: his shoulders, his ribs, his back. His jaw. The fluttering pulse at the base of his neck. I press my mouth there and taste the salt of his skin. The sweat I've been watching him work up all night. I press down against him, grinding my hips against his, and he gasps.

"I want to be inside of you," he says. "Is that—can we—"

"Yes."

Thank god this is the kind of silly, too-cool hotel that puts condoms in its minibar. Charlie keeps my gaze while he climbs out of bed, shimmies the rest of the way out of his pants and underwear, and retrieves one.

He moves himself inside of me gently but firmly, coaxing me open, and I embrace the loss of control. I let out a high, startled cry. It just feels *so good*.

Immediately, my cheeks go hot, and my eyes slam shut. Like if I can't see him, he won't be able to see what he's doing to me. Charlie pauses, and I can almost feel him weighing his options. Trying to decide what to do next. *You might only get this once*, I remind myself.

I open my eyes to find his gaze still on me, bright and serious. He brings his hand to my chin, gently tugs on my lip with his thumb, and whispers, "Thank you," as if I'm the one doing him a favor.

And then he starts to fuck me in earnest, his hips rocking against mine and our bodies climbing the mattress. And still he holds eye contact. Like he knows that I am doing everything I can to stay in this moment, to not let anything outside of the present, outside of the two of us, creep in.

I lose track of where I end and he begins. I let myself be

empty, except for him. I stop thinking about what this means or if we'll ever do it again. I have no strategy. I have no thoughts. I have just Charlie and the desire to make him come apart like I did. I squeeze against him and grab handfuls of his ass, palm his back, dig my nails into his biceps.

When he gets there, he bites down on my shoulder, hard enough to leave a mark. It feels like a claim being staked: *You are mine.*

I know he doesn't mean it, but I love the sensation all the same.

X

I can tell it's too early to be up, and yet, nonetheless, I'm awake. Jet lag insists that it's a decent hour, even though my phone informs me that it's not yet 7:00 a.m.

I lie still for a few moments, trying to make sense of everything that's happened in the last twenty-four hours. The wedding. Charlie singing to me. Charlie going down on me, and then fucking me, and then falling asleep holding me: my face pressed against his chest, his fingers still tangled in my hair.

We separated at some point in the night, but when I glance over, I see that he's still here. He's turned away from me, so my view is the breadth of his shoulders, the smooth skin of his back, the curve of his neck. I want to reach out and touch him—to make sure that he's as real as he was last night.

But then he'll wake up, and when he wakes up, there will probably be a conversation.

One I'm dreading having. Charlie is about to go on a whirlwind world press tour. He's back in the public eye for the first time in years. He has a chance for a fresh start—to make himself something other than "one of the guys from Mischief." The last thing he needs is the anchor of my reputation. Something or someone to answer for. To say nothing of the many reasons why I can't get more involved than I already am. This has to be a one-time thing.

Even knowing that, I don't regret it. I also can't help wishing that it was possible to have more.

On a less existential level, I also really have to pee, so I take a deep breath and carefully shimmy out of bed. I try to be as quiet as possible while I wash my hands and splash water on my face, but it's no use. By the time I get back, Charlie is lying on his side, facing me. Awake.

"Hey," he says. He looks sleepy but bright-eyed, taking in my naked skin. I feel simultaneously vulnerable and protected by the frankness of his gaze.

I figured Charlie would want to take advantage of the early hour to try to slip out of the hotel unnoticed, but his energy is still, calm. So I get back in bed. "Did you sleep OK?"

"Mmmm." He reaches for me, pulling me toward him, and I'm more than happy to go. There's something so simple about morning-after sex, when you're both already naked and there's nothing left to prove. The night's urgency is gone, but it's replaced by something slow and sweet and thick. Charlie strokes his fingers along my sides, a lazy caress, and sparks shoot across the skin he touches. I arch my back and push myself against his erection. I desperately want him to hold me in place, right here, right now, for just a little while longer.

But then the rattle of his alarm breaks our reverie.

"Fuck," Charlie says, rolling away to turn it off. "Fuck, fuck, fuck."

"Are you late?"

"No, but . . . I really should go. My plane is in a few hours."

He slides his hand along my hip one last time and plants a firm kiss on my forehead. Then he gets out of bed and starts pulling on his pants.

"Oh, I didn't realize your flight was this early. You didn't have to—" *stay*, I'm about to say, but Charlie just laughs.

"I wanted to." He sounds so . . . certain about it. Like there was never any question that a few more hours with me, asleep, was worth a rush in the morning.

I sit up in bed, letting the sheets pool around my body. With another man, I might feel self-conscious, but I *want* Charlie to see me right now. To return his confidence with my own. Something inside of me is cracking open—whatever I created to seal away any sense of *hope* or *want* after Cooper is crumbling into dust. Maybe this isn't just a one-night thing after all? Maybe—maybe—

Mischief Maya would have asked, I tell myself. So I gather my courage, "Does this mean you owe *me* one? For running out like this."

Charlie doesn't say anything. He just smirks, chews that bottom lip again, and gestures for me to come to him.

I stand. Morning sunlight streams through the sheer curtains and surrounds my naked body, warm and soft. Charlie pulls me to him for a long, slow kiss that leaves me seeing streaks behind my eyelids. When I pull away, he looks as dazed as I feel.

"You can have as much of me as you want, Maya," he promises.

It's hard to imagine a better sentence.

XI

I spend the rest of the day in a pleasant, well-fucked haze. I float through 405 traffic and the airport's long security line. Instead of working, I take a nap on the flight. When I wake up, just in time to deplane, I have a text from Kate: *Hey—can you send this to Charlie? Just wanted to make sure he's OK with what our photographer posted.* Followed by an Instagram link.

A picture of Charlie singing, I guess? Kate would have said *you and Charlie* if it involved both of us. She's even more protective of me than I am of myself.

I click and start scrolling through the photo carousel that pops up. I'm in the background of a few shots, but not doing anything interesting, just dancing and smiling. Enjoying the night. If you can see Charlie near me, it doesn't look anything other than incidental.

Then I get to the last slide. I was right that it's Charlie, up on stage, singing "Until It Rains." It's a video. But in it, you can see me there too.

Not my face. The photographer must have been standing five or ten feet behind me, so all you can make out is the back of my head, and the fall of my dress. I'm half in shadow. Still, it's hard to miss that Charlie is looking at me.

Not just that. The *way* he's looking at me.

I'm glad I'm sitting down, because I start to get dizzy. An array of scenarios—headlines, disasters—unspool in front of my eyes. It's a professional skill set to be able to game out possibilities and probabilities, but in the last year, what used to be my superpower has become my nightmare. A rush of memories overtakes me, more sensation than anything. Panic. Claustrophobia. The feeling of being watched, and judged, and exposed.

Do the research, I command myself. *Find out what the situation is. Stay in control.*

My breathing gets shallow as I scroll down to the comments. Part of me already knows what I'm going to find.

Fans are a community. Fans are a force. And fans are also a detective unit. Plenty of them still monitor every video their fave—in this case, Charlie—appears in, and they'll find it regardless of whether he's tagged. And of course, they're itching to know who Charlie was making eyes at while he sang.

I watch in real time, over spotty tarmac Wi-Fi, as they figure it out. *She tagged @kate_block as the bride, but her account is private, so I googled Kate + "Charlie Blake" and "Mischief." Looks like she used to run a fan group back in the day?*

Oh shit, she used to run that group with Maya McPherson LOL wouldn't it be epic if this was her??

Honestly kind of looks like her? But then I guess it could be any white girl with red-brown hair.

Ummmm OK but look at the back right of the third pic in the carousel . . .

One of those innocuous photos of me. I'm on the dance floor; Charlie isn't even in the frame. The flash picks out my freckles in stark relief, and my body is a series of curves in the silk of my dress. My hands are in the air. I look like I'm having the time of my life. I think I was.

Guys but like . . . that IS Maya McPherson?

Who is she?

Links to the stories about Cooper's cheating start popping into the thread.

Any sense that I might be able to control the situation collapses. I watch my phone screen blankly for a few minutes, a bright blue scroll of information, before I can make my numb fingers shut it down.

It's only then that I realize that I'm on the verge of fully hyperventilating. My breath isn't just catching in my throat and then releasing again; it's stuck now, struggling to force its way in and out of my chest. My lungs work like a bellows, but I can't get enough air. A trickle of cold sweat runs down my back as I hunt through my bag for my wallet, which contains an emergency Xanax for moments just like this one. My teeth are chattering with fear by the time I get it into my mouth.

I slip it under my tongue, and its chalky, bitter taste calms me instantly. Before the divorce, I'd never had a panic attack. Now I've had enough to know that there's no point in trying to ride it out, especially in public. My mouth is so dry, but it's several long minutes before I can unclench my hands and reach for a water bottle to wash its aftertaste out of my mouth.

By the time it's my turn to grab my carry-on, it starts to kick in. It takes ten or fifteen miles an hour off of my racing thoughts and sands down the edges of my panic. I know I should do a breathing exercise. Unplug, anchor myself. Et cetera. I promise myself I'll do the necessary self-care when I'm at home. For now, I'm still in self-preservation mode.

So I force myself to disassociate. Pretend I'm not the subject of this debacle, but the client. What would I advise someone else to do, if her job and sanity were on the line like this?

I pick up my phone again. Hands still shaking. Kate has already texted *Shit, just saw the comments. She's taking it down.*

It's probably better to leave it now, I write back.

Then I do what I do best. I come up with a plausible story. I start a mental list of a few media contacts to reach out to to see if anyone is interested in hearing it. Bait a hook. Test a reaction. Come up with something that might stick.

Teresa doesn't give me much time. She calls just as I'm walking into my apartment. "Hi," I say. "Listen—"

She cuts me off immediately. "Is this, or is this not, exactly what we talked about before I hired you. This big reputation of yours."

The Xanax keeps panic at bay, but it can't do anything about guilt, or dread, or shame. My racing thoughts are replaced by venom-induced paralysis that makes me want to freeze in time. Just stop living, somehow. My stomach coils and twists. I don't know if I've ever felt so small. "Yes."

"What else do I need to know?"

The romantic fantasy of my night with Charlie seems so

tawdry in this light. I resent the shit out of having to tell her anything about my personal life, but I also know she needs to know everything so we can assess the situation and decide how to handle it. My iron will has pushed me through so many impossible situations in my life. I beg it to stick with me for just a little longer. Let me sound professional while I talk to Teresa. I'll have a breakdown immediately after, I swear.

"We kissed," I admit. "At the wedding. I went home with him. I don't think anyone saw that stuff, but obviously I'm not sure."

"Maya." The disappointment in Teresa's voice is palpable. "You have to know this was a stupid thing to do."

Part of me wants to remind both of us that I was off the clock. That this shouldn't matter. But we both know that *fair* doesn't apply here. And it does matter. A lot. "I know. But I've already talked to some reporters, and they said—"

"You talked to reporters? Who gave you permission to do that?"

I try to keep the ice out of my voice when I say, "I was doing my due diligence, Teresa. I need to know what they're hearing in order to know where we're at."

"And?"

Deep breath. There's a way out of this. "Leah's a stylist. One of the brides. So if you're OK with it, I'll call those people back. Have them quote me as a source close to the situation. And we say that Charlie and Leah are old friends. He was a wedding guest; of course I introduced myself. He sang the song as a gift to Kate and Leah. And I impressed him so much with my UBI pitch that, look, now he's going to be supporting your campaign! It manages any potential scandal. It lets us ride the publicity a little bit. And it doesn't fuck with our plans to have him speak in three weeks."

Teresa sighs, and then there's a long silence. "You're smart," she says. "I have to give you that. And I want you to succeed, Maya. But you have to stop shooting yourself in the foot with your personal life." A pause. "Let's see what turns up between now and tomorrow morning. If no one has anything more salacious, we go with your story, and you keep your job. But if this does become a real scandal—if you make me look stupid for bringing you on board . . ."

Charlie's promise from this morning echoes in my ears. *You can have as much of me as you want.* This weekend, I got off track and let myself believe maybe I could have him, and this too. Everything.

But Charlie is basically a stranger. There's no guarantee of a future there. This is my career, which I've been fighting for since I was barely out of my teens. I'm not letting these adolescent feelings—or anything—fuck it up. I *will* win back what Cooper took from me.

I deliberately don't think about what I might lose in the process.

It's the only way through this.

"I understand," I tell her.

"Good," she says and hangs up without a goodbye.

Then I sit down on the floor. I've held it together for as long as humanly possible, and it's a relief to curl into a ball and let myself weep.

I spend the next twenty-four hours glued to my couch, unable to will myself out of my plane clothes. My smartwatch keeps pinging me about my heart rate. I finally just take it off.

Charlie calls. I don't answer. I need to find a way to put a guard up before I do. If I talk to him now, I'll be looking to him for comfort, something I need to be finding absolutely anywhere else. Instead I shoot him a text, telling him I'll catch up with him soon.

I have an interview to do tomorrow, he says. *Should I tell my team to make you off-limits?*

I put my phone down and massage my head where a seemingly permanent tension headache has taken up residence between my temples. I know Charlie's just trying to make sure he's following my lead here, but I don't want to be managing my own strategic response to this, let alone his. Given the time difference, and that I'm relying on Teresa to give me the OK to plant my story, I can't guarantee what the right line will be when he and this reporter talk. So *yes, please*, I say.

The headlines roll in anyway. Charlie was already back in the news again, because of the single, and linking his name with mine seems to garner clicks. In the absence of an official narrative, the rumor is that Anna Wintour set us up at the Met Gala last year, which is hilarious given I have never been to the Met Gala. But who needs the truth when you have the comments section?

Once we've gotten through Monday without any other news leaking, Teresa gives me the go-ahead to call reporters and give them my spin.

Which means I have to stop avoiding Charlie. Having to tell him the plan adds insult to injury, salt in my wounds. The time zones between us are impossible, so I just hit *call* and hope he's awake.

"Hey," he says, groggy, and I have a flash of waking up next to him. How much I wanted to do it more than once. "How are you doing? Where are you? Is there something new?" He can't seem to decide where to put his focus.

"Nothing new," I assure him.

The rustle of cloth—probably sheets—as he rearranges himself. "Are you OK, Maya?" There's real concern in his voice, and I want to curl up inside of it. To let myself be human, and hurt.

But I'm basically being held together by wet glue. I'm too fragile to be real with him. So instead I say, "I've been worse!" with a brave little laugh. It probably doesn't sound very convincing.

"I'm so sorry," he says.

"*You* didn't do anything."

There's silence on the other end, and I can tell he's weighing the validity of my statement. "I'm making your life complicated. I don't think you need the complication."

I take a deep breath. "You're making my *work* complicated." I explain about Teresa; I sketch the story I want to sell to the press. "I have a friend at *People* who will call me 'a source close to the situation,'" I say. "You don't have to do anything except not deny it if anyone asks. And . . . ideally, you'd still come speak about UBI. But that's entirely up to you."

"Of course," Charlie says. "Of course I will. And when I see you we'll . . ."

"We'll be acquaintances," I tell him. My tone is curt. "Polite. Professional."

A faint sound. Maybe him swallowing. "OK."

I press the heels of my hands into my eyes until I see stars. The solo album was supposed to be an opportunity for him to do this on his own terms. And now I'm asking him to lie for me.

"I know this is not the way you wanted to do things this time around," I say. "I'm sorry."

"I've had worse publicity." I know he doesn't mean it that way, but the sentence stings all the same. As if I'm just another optics crisis in a long line of them, another little public mess he has to manage. Less embarrassing than the time Ramsey drunkenly started spouting off about the IRA at the BRITs, at least. Should I offer to coordinate with his team directly, I wonder? Since I'm the reason they're dealing with this at all?

But Charlie interrupts my thoughts when he asks, quietly, "Are you sure you're OK?"

Which is honestly maybe worse.

"I'm OK," I say as firmly as I can muster.

"OK," he echoes.

I get off the phone as fast as possible. I could barely lie to him once. I know I won't be able to do it again.

XII

The next three weeks pass in a blur. I work like a machine, diligent and driven. After hours, I engage in every mood-regulating, head-clearing activity that my therapist prescribed after the divorce: yoga, meditation, walks where I don't look at my phone. I cut out alcohol and clean out my closet. I wipe down my countertops and drink lots of water. I'm a wellness influencer's wet dream. I recite dumb-but-wise mantras to myself. *Be where your feet are* is a big one.

Gabe handles the balance of Charlie's speech prep. He doesn't ask me anything about what happened between us in LA, and I'm impossibly grateful. Every time I have to repeat the lie that we had only just met—that it was friendly, that nothing happened—I feel like a child who misbehaved and is trying to hide it. I hate acting like I've done something wrong by giving into attraction, and I hate pretending he means nothing to me.

The night of the debate, I open up social media to find people are tweeting Mischief GIFs at the campaign's account, wishing Teresa good luck. I know they mean well by it. It's still hard to watch.

I don't take another Xanax, but I know exactly where they

are in my bag. This is always the hardest part for me anyway. When we're strategizing and planning, I'm in control. And then there's this moment where the candidate goes out on their own, and all I can do is wait and see what I'll have to spin in the aftermath.

To her credit, Teresa is near-flawless. She's self-assured but also warm and humble; she's sharp when she needs to be without ever crossing the line to what will earn her the badge of "shrewish." I've been working with Teresa the human being for the last few months, and it's fascinating to watch her become Teresa the politician. *I'd vote for her*, I think abstractly.

When a question about economic strategy comes up, she doesn't hesitate. "I will be the kind of governor who's not afraid to pursue big, bold ideas," she says. "Starting with addressing poverty with universal basic income. A stipend that we give to *everyone* to spend on what they need. Because some people need rent money, and some need diapers. Some have to pay the internet bill so that their kids can get online to do homework. And the fact is, it shouldn't be the government's role to decide what's most important to each family—it's our job to ensure each family has enough. This is a flexible solution that requires minimal bureaucracy and has been shown again and again to have maximal effect."

There's a smattering of applause in the room, and for the first time in days, I realize, I'm smiling like I mean it. This has been such a fucking mess. But if Teresa wins—if we enact this legislation—it could all be worth it too.

That night, as I'm getting in bed, I see a text. Charlie. *Just watched the debate. Looks like it went well. Good motivation for tomorrow.* It's so . . . friendly. Normal.

I appreciate him breaking the ice and setting the tone for the day ahead. Now I just have to make it through twenty-four hours without incident, and Charlie Blake will be out of my life, just as quickly as he entered it.

XIII

It's exactly the kind of spring morning that makes you think winter can't possibly have been as bad as you remember. Standing in front of the high school where we're setting up for the press conference, it's a touch too warm for my usual Serious Person drag—a sharply cut dark-green suit that I had a menswear tailor make for me a few years ago. I slip the jacket off my shoulders and hang it over the back of a folding chair. I let myself pause for just a moment, turning my face up toward the sun. The event doesn't start for another hour, but I overdid it with the coffee, and my heart is already beating too fast. I'm nervously fidgeting with the sapphire studs in my ears, the same ones I wore to Kate's wedding.

Of course, that's when I hear his voice.

"Maya?"

My eyes snap open. Charlie is standing right in front of me, as infuriatingly handsome as ever. He's wearing a sober navy suit and a tie, and I think about what it would feel like to wrap the length of silk around my fist, because despite myself, I am still me and he is still him. We awkwardly hug—more like a mutual pat on each other's shoulders—and if it wasn't for my unfortunate grip on reality, I could almost embrace it as some sort of sexy "let's pretend we're strangers" role-play.

"Any trouble getting in?"

"None," he says. But he looks as uncertain as I feel.

What a relief. If he'd rolled up, cool and casual, my cracked heart might have actually broken. I can't help being glad this isn't easy for him either. That we both feel off-balance, like we missed a step somewhere between *you can have as much of me as you want* and *just kidding, that never happened*.

"Can I get you anything?" I ask, trying to smooth out the moment. "Water? Coffee?"

"Klonopin," he deadpans. We both laugh, and whatever it is between us snaps into place. I feel like I feel with him. Natural. Easy.

"You're gonna be great."

He raises a skeptical eyebrow. "Mmhmm."

"Even just talking, in the hotel room—" I shake my head— "You could have done this then, honestly."

"Thank you." Charlie nods, and I have the sense that he's physically forcing himself to take the compliment. When he looks up, our eyes meet, and all I can think is *danger*.

I don't look away.

"It's really good to see you," Charlie says. "Even if—I know things are—" He laughs and gives up on that sentence. "Anyway. I'm glad you're . . . OK."

"It is. Good," I agree. And then I hustle him off to our events coordinator before I can say anything even more ill-advised, like *I missed you*. Or *You're the last thing I think about at night and the first thing I think about in the morning and probably the only thing swimming through my head when I'm asleep too.*

Charlie is our last speaker of the day, and I can tell people are getting a little restless by the time he steps up to the mic. When people see him, though, they snap to attention. Photographers' lenses *click, click, click* as fast as they can.

Charlie leans over the podium and offers us all a smile. "I'm Charlie Blake," he says. He looks as polished as ever, but his voice has a tiny, nervous wobble. He glances down at his papers, then looks up again.

The pause is long enough for one of the reporters to get bold. "Charlie, c'mon. Give us something. Are you dating Maya McPherson? Is that why you're here?"

I freeze. My brain, my heart, my lungs—every single organ in my body braces. Teresa's fury is a furnace, blazing against my back, but I can't even make myself turn my head to meet her eye.

Charlie doesn't so much as flinch. When he angles himself toward the mic, he's almost menacing. "No," he says. His voice is low with controlled anger. "I'm not dating Ms. McPherson. I wasn't planning to discuss this, but let's clear that up. We were introduced by mutual friends, and I was impressed and inspired by her passion for universal basic income, which is a topic I also happen to care about deeply."

The guy who asked the question looks appropriately cowed. As for me, all I can think about is how insanely hot Charlie is when he's righteously pissed off, especially on my behalf. He usually seems like he's trying to shrug off his celebrity, and I'm charmed by that. But it's also sexy to see him own the sway he has over people, using it to disarm a cocky reporter with a few well-aimed words.

Charlie is in his element now, and my heart clenches with pride as he turns to the rest of the crowd. "I think we can level with each other. I'm here because—my name is the reason a lot of *you* are here, am I right?"

There's a knowing laugh from the assembled press corps. They're charmed. Anyone who didn't show up for him is here for him now.

"But I'm up here, out of my element, because this is a cause that could change lives. And I think it's worth bringing attention to it. So if there aren't any other questions about my personal life . . ."

No one has the balls to interrupt him this time.

"I'm Charlie Blake," Charlie repeats. "And if you know my name, it's probably because I was in a band called Mischief in the early 2000s. We were very lucky, and for a while, we were very successful."

He tells the story of his dad's accident again. When we talked in the hotel room, he was sad. Mournful. Now he keeps the edge of anger from his conversation with the reporter in his voice. The frustration of what was taken from his family. It only makes his delivery more powerful. There's a fire in his eyes, and I can feel myself standing taller. It's a welcome reminder of why I do this.

"When I became wealthy, I vowed to give back to my

community, right here in Massachusetts," Charlie says. He's in the groove, and I know he has everyone's attention right where he wants it. "I started an after-school music program, which I've been funding for over a decade now. I've sent millions of dollars to various programs to help kids in my county buy backpacks, and lunches, and Halloween costumes.

"Every year, it's a reminder of something I already knew. Of something I experienced myself as a kid: The system is broken. It's grounded in inequality that concentrates money in the hands of people like me, which is to say, white men who either came into it systemically or, in my case, through dumb luck. I cherish getting to make those contributions, but why should *I* decide what poor kids need, or what they get? Music changed my life, so I fund a music program. My dad loved Halloween, and I love knowing that kids get to have at least one night of fun and candy a year. But what if I had other priorities? What would those kids get? How would their lives be different?

"If you're thinking I shouldn't be up here talking about this today: you're right. I shouldn't be. I also shouldn't be in a position where my money makes choices for other people's families. They should have their own money, that they can spend in ways that are right for them. They know their needs much better than I—or anybody else—ever could."

Charlie pauses, straightens his spine. I tilt my chin up.

"I'm here today because, whether or not they should, people listen when I talk. And so if you hear this clip on YouTube or TikTok, or read a snippet of a speech on Twitter. If you've ever cared about my music, or my clothing line, or read a magazine article about my love life—please. Care about this as much as you cared about that. And vote for Teresa Powell for governor of Massachusetts this November."

He clicks off his microphone, and the next speaker crosses the stage. It takes everything I have not to leap to my feet and applaud.

XIV

I'm still recovering from Charlie's speech as the press conference wraps up, and our team starts folding up the chairs and unplugging the equipment. I should be chasing the journalists, doing follow-up, but I need a minute, so I slip past them to the school's main entrance. They let us use their bathrooms instead of bringing in port-a-potties, so the doors are unlocked.

And there he is, Charlie, leaning against a row of lockers in the empty hallway of a public high school. Honestly, it would be so much easier on me if he'd quit with the Jordan Catalano cosplay. He's jacket-less now, sleeves rolled, tie discarded. The clout that rolled off him in waves when he was on stage has dissipated; he looks rumpled and casual. Intimate. He raises his hand in greeting.

A grin splits my face. I'm too giddy to pretend right now. "You fucking killed it."

He grins back. "I was so nervous, and then—that question— but it kind of helped, weirdly. I was too mad to be nervous. Like, what is there to worry about if this is the caliber of the people I'm talking to?"

"I should have warned you about the idiocy of the press corps."

"I know for next time." He gets serious again. "Thank you, though. I'm glad I did it. That I pushed myself, and just . . . said everything I said. I know you know this, but you are excellent at your job."

He says that last part with so much conviction that it makes me suddenly and painfully aware of just how much self-doubt I've been harboring, a realization that brings me to the brink of tears. I've become so accustomed to swallowing the words I want to say, and I can only imagine how good it would feel to let them all out. To tell Charlie all about how I wanted my comeback to be about making a difference, but I'm scared I'm getting wrapped up in my own bullshit—and DC's bullshit— again. How I used to know I was excellent at my job, but these days I don't feel sure of much at all. Instead, I reach out to where my hair has been pulled back all day and let it tumble down, hoping it hides whatever's on my face. "I'm really glad you did it too," I say.

But he's not blind. He steps in close to me and touches his index finger to the bottom of my chin. I let him guide my face up. I blink once, then again.

Charlie is close enough that I can see the crow's-feet at the corners of his eyes. The curve of his mouth. He's plenty close to kiss. I draw in a long breath, and it comes out shaky.

"I was going to ask if you were really OK," Charlie says into the hush between us. "I know you said . . . but I've been worried about you. And I know we're not supposed to say things like this to each other. But I . . . I'm distracted."

"Yeah," I say. Unsure of what part of his statement I'm responding to, exactly.

The school doors bang open, and I step back so fast I almost trip over my own feet. Thank god when I look up, it's Gabe looking at me.

He does me the sort of favor that he's adept at doing. "I was hoping I'd find both of you together," he says, doubling down on nonchalance by scrolling through his inbox. "Teresa was really impressed with Charlie. She wants to take you out to dinner and discuss an encore."

I already have plans tonight, to see a couple of friends from college while I'm in town. I figured I'd need a distraction, and drink, after having to see Charlie and say goodbye to him in short order.

Besides, it feels a little shitty to have been called to the carpet for hanging out with Charlie . . . only to now be asked to do it on purpose. But only because Teresa has decided that it benefits her.

Not that I'm about to pitch a fit over the idea of spending more time with him.

Charlie glances at me. I nod very slightly. Gabe knows me well enough to notice, but thankfully, he would never let on.

"I'd love that," Charlie says. "I just have to be on a plane at ten p.m.—can we do something early?"

I spend the rest of the day dashing off emails and barely find time to reapply deodorant before Gabe drives himself and me to Woods Hill for our work dinner for four.

"Charlie seems nice," he observes mildly once we're on our way.

I lean my head against the window. "How obvious is it?"

"Oh, you're both total goners." Gabe laughs and reaches over to ruffle my hair. I duck out of the way just in time. My stomach clenches on the word *both*. Are we really? Both?

"We're friends," is what I say out loud.

"Friends who fucked."

"But just once!"

"You're not gonna invite him home after this for a nightcap? Another late-night strategy session? Please."

I want to do that. I want it so badly that for a second, I can't breathe.

Gabe glances over at me. "What? Did I make it weird, interrupting you guys back there?"

"No. You heard him—he has a flight. And even if he didn't, it's just . . . it's not gonna happen. I can't risk it with Teresa. I'm on thin ice with her as it is."

"So keep it a secret."

"I tried that! Turns out Charlie is famous!"

"Him serenading you at your friend's wedding was your idea of *secret*?"

It's like the devil on my shoulder has come to life and taken his seat behind the wheel of an Audi sedan. When he says it like that, it sounds like it would be so easy to get it right this time.

"I can't do it all again, Gabe," I tell him. "Getting called out like that—having people talk about me—it really fucked with my head. *I* need to focus on the campaign. There can't be anything else right now."

"OK. OK. I'll leave it." Gabe sighs, and then a wicked smile overtakes his face. "Does this mean I can flirt with him at dinner?"

When I see Teresa at the hostess stand, I clock the tiredness around her eyes. If my schedule on this campaign is tough, hers is a nightmare—she's still holding down her House job in addition to trying to win this office. I just hope that getting the debate and press conference done has lifted some weight off her shoulders.

As we walk to the table, she touches my arm, and I fall into step with her. "Thank you for getting Charlie on board," she says. "Our digital team says our numbers are through the roof on his speech. That dog whistle for his fans to post about it on social was sharp. Nicely done."

"I'm glad it all worked out."

She pauses just slightly, and I pause too. "I know I was hard on you," she says. "But I . . . I know what it's like, being a woman in politics. I don't want to see you make stupid mistakes. You have a lot of potential. You should live up to it."

I'm thirty-five, not twenty-two, I want to tell her. I am too old to be patronized like this and too young to have bought into *Lean In.* I don't just have potential; I have success. I realize Charlie's words from earlier are already seeping into my bloodstream: I *am* excellent at my job, and I do know it. But there's not much to be gained from turning this into a soapbox moment, so I try to appreciate the gesture for what it is—her trying to soften up with me. I give her my most gracious "Thank you."

Charlie is already in our booth, and I can almost taste the

old-fashioned in front of him on my own tongue. Gabe slides in to sit next to him, and I'm grateful that I won't have the proximity of our thighs clouding my thoughts all night.

"I have to admit," Teresa says, drinks order in. "When Maya first brought your name up, Charlie, I was a little skeptical. But you were a force up there. Have you ever thought about getting into politics?"

"God no," he says. "You can ask Maya—I had to be coaxed into doing this in the first place." He grins, just for me, like we share a little secret, even though the two other people at our table know more than half of it.

Gabe shrugs. "If you change your mind, I saw at least three articles speculating about it this afternoon."

My mind immediately races off to find the angle. It'd be a tough sell; Charlie has his hard-luck origin story, but then he was a pop star, and for the last six years, he's been selling $700 sweaters and winning CFDA awards. This speech would be a good start, but you'd really have to—

Charlie interrupts my train of thought with a more sober answer. "I respect what you guys do too much," he says. "I'm a person with political opinions, but I've also spent half my life surrounded by people whose job it is to tell me I have good ideas. I know better than to trust my own ego with real power."

It must be so strange to always wonder if anyone has ever told you the truth about yourself. Charlie rakes a hand through his hair, and my eyes track the motion. The flex of his forearm; the glow of the scar right near his elbow that I know, from my embarrassingly encyclopedic Mischief knowledge, happened while horsing around with Chris on tour.

"Well, I was hoping you wouldn't mind lending us your star power on the campaign again," Teresa says.

Charlie glances at me again, an instinctive little check-in. I wish I could pause the moment and say everything I'm thinking— that he should, because he's good at this, and he deserves to use his voice. That he can't, because if I have to spend more time around him, forced to look but not touch, I might lose my mind. That I want him to, and I don't want him to, in perfectly equal measure.

In the end, though, there's only one question: What's good for the campaign? And I know that answer. I give him a tiny nod.

Charlie turns to Teresa. "What were you thinking?"

Teresa lays out her plan over appetizers. She has a big fund-raiser coming up at the end of the summer, and she wants Charlie to headline. It's a smart play: he's still a new solo artist, so there will be plenty of draw from people who haven't seen him perform since he was a teenager. He can do his speech again. Maybe bring along a celeb friend or two.

I expect Charlie to be wary about being taken advantage of. But he warms to the idea immediately, and we have just enough time to hash out the basic logistics, some potential asks, before Charlie has to catch his plane.

"Maya, you want a ride?" Gabe asks as we're leaving.

"No, but thank you so much!"

He gives me the most loving eye roll but doesn't call my bluff. Teresa's husband is already waiting out front to pick her up, which leaves me and Charlie alone on the sidewalk.

I can't say I wasn't hoping it would happen like this. "I feel like I keep saying thank you," I tell him. "So one more time: you're really helping us out so much."

"And I keep telling you, I'm happy to do it." He glances at his phone, and I can see a driver's location on the screen, inching closer and closer. "But I just want to double-check—this is OK, right? Me doing this? If you change your mind, I can—"

"We're fine," I assure him. "I mean, I'm fine. If you're fine."

"I'm fine."

I watch on his phone and in real life as his driver rounds the corner and pulls toward us.

"We'll be friends," I lie, as if I can possibly be friends with someone who makes me ache every time I look at him.

"Friends." Charlie rolls the word around in his mouth, not quite sure how he feels about its taste.

"Or just be professional. That works too."

The car's waiting. It's brand new, sleek and black. The kind you get driven around in, if you're a rock star. "No," Charlie says. "We can—friends. Let's do that."

"OK."

He moves a half step toward me, but then stops himself. The phantom feeling of a hug—his body pressed against mine, even just for a second. I shiver in his absence.

"We'll talk," Charlie says.

"We'll talk," I agree.

He doesn't even have to touch the car's door; it opens for him, and his real life swallows him up again.

XV

We don't talk. Or, he doesn't text me, and I don't text him. I have no idea what I would say if I did. What I even thought I meant by suggesting friendship to him. Every time I so much as think his name, I feel mildly insane, like I'm fifteen again and drunk on the sensation of a crush. So I try not to think about him as much as possible.

There is work to do, and as far as he's involved with that, I communicate with his assistant, Merrill. She's efficient and to the point. We put Teresa's fundraiser on Charlie's calendar, book his travel, consult with our people about how long he'll play (a three-song set) and whether he'll do any formal speaking (not really), consult with his people about his needs and who he'll bring in support (a solid set of celeb pals).

I track an uptick in coverage of UBI: *Teen Vogue* does a big feature talking to kids whose families have participated in pilots, and the *Boston Globe* runs a three-part investigative feature on the history and future of the idea. Politicians running for other positions in other states and cities start to mention test programs as a possibility, and they cite Teresa when they do.

I'm also watching my own professional stock start to rise.

Climbers who were ignoring me at parties are excited to see me again; I get a few calls from people trying to woo me away from Teresa's campaign and onto their own. I let myself be just a little smug about refusing each invitation. Teresa took a chance on me, and I'm not going to bail on her now.

See, I tell myself. *This is working. It's going to be worth it.* The promise almost makes up for how rocked I am every time I catch one of Charlie's songs playing in a coffee shop or see his face on Instagram. The way my heart lurches when I get an email from Merrill.

It's a steamy Wednesday night in June, and I'm at home finishing up some last pieces of work when Kate texts me: *You're watching Fallon tonight?*

Am I?

Charlie's the musical guest!!

I knew about the appearance, but I had completely missed that it was tonight.

I've been doing nothing but work lately, so I decide to make a night out of it. And by "make a night," I mean I go to a nearby wine store and pick up a bottle and one of the fancy ginger-flecked chocolate bars they sell. I grab a tub of olives and a hunk of soft cheese. I sign up for a free YouTube TV trial, and I'm stupidly satisfied with myself for figuring out how to stream it just as Jimmy's starting his opening monologue.

I get a little nostalgic. Except for the wine and the quality of my snacks, I could be in my childhood living room, staying up past my bedtime to watch a member of Mischief make a public appearance. Back then, there would have been a tape whirring in the VCR, recording every minute. Now it'll all be clipped and GIFed for me five minutes after it airs.

In the lead-up to Charlie's entrance, I'm anxious the way I used to be at concerts: hyped up and restless. When he actually steps on stage, I let myself reenact the role of lovestruck teen and fling an arm over my eyes and let out a groan. He's wearing head-to-toe Char: the thinnest cream knit tucked into a pair of wide-leg suit pants. His hair has grown out since the last time I saw him; it's just short of shaggy—boyish, a nice contrast to the faint circles under his eyes. He stretches out an arm across the back of his chair, and I have to look away from the way the material of his shirt reveals the curve of his biceps. I set my laptop on the coffee table.

Telling Jimmy a story about how he and Devin's daughter almost burned the house down the night he wrote the song "Longer Gone," Charlie is peak charming. "I didn't think marshmallows were *that* flammable," he laments, and the audience cracks up. He's doing the thing he's been trained for since he was a teenager, and the ease with which he navigates the attention on him is hot, especially having seen the way that self-doubt creeps in for him just like it does for me. For everyone I know.

But then, "You've also gotten pretty political lately," Jimmy says, and I stiffen automatically. I trust Charlie knows his talking points, but we haven't workshopped this at all. Given him statistics to cite. Vetted his answers for a late-night audience. I really wish he would have given us the heads-up that this was on the table.

And of course, I wonder, Is Jimmy going to ask about UBI? Or about me?

Charlie sits up a little straighter, crosses his legs. He doesn't look surprised. Just determined, the same as he did before he laid into that reporter at the press conference. "I've always been political. I've recently started being public about my politics."

"OK, fair enough," Jimmy concedes. "Why did you pick this campaign? And this particular cause?"

Charlie angles himself slightly, so that it seems like he's addressing the TV viewers and Jimmy at the same time. "Honestly, this wasn't something I was looking for," he says. "When the campaign first approached me, I was scared. A lot of people like their celebrities to . . . how does the saying go? Shut up and sing. And I didn't want to be one of those people who mouths off for the hell of it." He looks down at his hands, and then back at the camera. "But I'm a person, right? So I'm trying to be more open about what's important to me, as a person."

"But you'll still sing for us, right?" Jimmy heckles. The audience laughs dutifully.

Charlie leans his elbows on the desk separating the two of them with mock flirtatiousness. "I'm here to make your teenage dreams come true, Jimmy. But I do want to say this before I shut up. Being able to learn more about universal basic income has been a real privilege. I'm also partnering with HeadCount to have voter registration at all of my shows this summer. I know a lot of my crowd is a little older, but hey—better late than never, right?"

"I guess you'd know a little something about that. And speaking of better late than never—are we all ready for a taste of Charlie's first solo album?"

I have a text from Kate. *Damn*, it says. *You really did a number on him, didn't you.*

He cares about the work, I respond.

MAYA MCPHERSON! BOTH CAN BE TRUE! WHEN WILL YOU START ENJOYING THIS!!!

I roll my eyes, but I can't help thinking that Kate is kind of right. The pop star of my dreams is on stage in New York, talking up UBI like it's his own single. And though he looks like he oozes confidence, I know that this is a huge leap for him—one I helped him take.

I pour myself another half glass of wine and let myself imagine, for a minute, what it would have been like if things were different between us right now. If he could have asked me to come to New York to see this in person. If he could have let me know it was happening at all.

I told him I wanted to be friends, and a friend would text him in this moment. And if I let it go by, well, then the moment will have passed. I reach for my phone: *You were great.*

I consider everything I could type next, and instead, I hit *send*.

XVI

The next morning, I wake up to a picture taken through the rainy window of a car. *Thank you*, Charlie wrote back. Then: *Wheels down in London. I was better at fighting jet lag when I was seventeen.*

I can't contain my glee. I sit up in bed, back against my headboard, grinning like an idiot. *Can't you get some good drugs to help?*

What I wouldn't give for a simple American cold brew, he responds while I'm brushing my teeth. *People keep trying to offer me tea.*

When do you get to sleep next?

When I'm dead.

Well, your Fallon performance is doing numbers. I woke up to like fifteen emails from people asking how I got you to do that, I tell him as I pack my work bag.

And? What's your secret?

It's like he's in the room with me; I can imagine exactly how he'd sound, saying those words. The look he'd give me to go along with them. I feel it right between my legs.

Not a very friendly way to be thinking. I type, *The secret is, you're perfect.* I delete it. I type, *The secret is you are good at what you do.*

Tell that to my manager. She says I shouldn't have had real milk in my latte and now my voice sounds froggy.

I spare a moment of sympathy for that woman. Charlie is so down-to-earth most of the time, but I'm sure he has his moments—like when he insists on dairy on a performance day, for instance. I don't say that, though. *Congrats on finally getting your hands on coffee??*

I have my ways. You may recall I crashed a wedding not that long ago—coffee is a comparative cakewalk.

I barely register the mixed feelings I should have about the memory of that night.

Oh, I recall, I can't help flirting back. My face hurts from smiling at my phone, trying to convey across an ocean how happy I am to be talking to him like this, first thing in the morning, offhand and intimate.

Good. BTW you had good instincts about "Until It Rains" that night. I performed it on Howard Stern earlier in the week and he's always had a soft spot for it.

I pause doing my makeup to reply. *Did you know that Christine Todd Whitman named a rest stop in New Jersey after Howard Stern in exchange for his endorsement of her run for governor?*

Should I start scheduling some site visits on I-95?

I'm just saying the hospitality rider your team sent over for the fundraiser seemed a little tame in comparison.

And then we just . . . keep talking. Charlie sends me updates about his favorite French bakery (still sublime) and the stylist who tries to dye his grays without asking permission first. I keep him updated on the sad muffins I'm eating at various meetings and the tally of how many times I send emails that say, "Just following up on this!" in a twenty-four-hour period.

It's chitchat—aside from the mention of the wedding night, it's actual just-friends stuff. I open up a little about work. Charlie's involvement with the campaign has been really helpful, but UBI isn't polling as well as I'd like. And despite our little breakthrough, Teresa is getting harder and harder to pin down as the campaign wears on. Which I know is par for the course with candidates—the closer we get to election day, the more there is for her to do. But combined with the numbers I see on my desk each week, I can't help feeling like I'm being shut out, slowly but surely.

Still want me to do the fundraiser though? Charlie asks after I text him from the office at 9:00 p.m., trying to see if I can nab Teresa in person, since she's been ignoring my emails.

Of course! I write back. Then, because I had lunch too early and I'm starving and grouchy and not thinking straight, I add, *Seeing you is basically the only thing I'm looking forward to at this point.*

Charlie doesn't respond immediately. I wish I could unsend my message, but I can only panic. My thoughts ping-pong between *that was way too much* and *we talk all the time—of course I want to see him.*

But what if he's with someone else? Aside from people like me messing with it, he's fairly skilled at keeping his private life private. I have no idea what his hookup habits are like these days, and it's hard to imagine him as priestly.

I realize I'm spiraling and put my phone face down and open up my laptop. It's only 6:00 p.m. Pacific; I can probably still catch some enterprising West Coast journalists at this hour. On top of trying to thread the UBI messaging just right, we're also looking for opportunities to raise Teresa's profile in general. Her opponent has been in politics since before she was born, so we're fighting an uphill battle with name recognition, and I have plenty of hounding to do.

An hour passes before I look at my phone again. Charlie has texted. *I'm looking forward to seeing you too.*

I close my eyes, and the words play on repeat. His phrasing is polite, but there's a chance that he misses me like I miss him.

Then he sends, *What are you up to right now?*

Still at work. I send him a little picture of my desk, which is a study in organized chaos, covered in sample mailers and data printouts.

Meanwhile, I'm trying to get myself out of bed. He adds a picture too: a selfie, taken from above. His hair is disheveled, and one bare arm is thrown over his face. It's a blurry shot, barely composed, but my throat goes dry. The ease and intimacy of it. How closely it recalls the actual experience of lying in bed next to him, that one morning when I could tuck myself under his arm and kiss the hollow of his throat. Press a palm against his stomach. Cause his breath to quicken for me.

He can't tell I'm biting my lip when I write back, *Keeping those rock star hours.*

I'm supposed to go to a party tonight. I don't want to.

Do you have to?

It's a work thing.

I raise an eyebrow at my phone. *Your work remains much more fun than mine.*

I guess.

It's after ten now; in all likelihood, Teresa is home, with her husband and son. I take a deep breath, flick the top button on my shirt open, and then the one below it. The effect is hardly scandalous, but it makes the resulting selfie look a little less like a business headshot, and more like I've been working all day, but I'm about to let my hair down. Like I'm too tired to be professional anymore. Which is the truth.

Which one of us looks like we're having more fun? I ask.

Another long pause. My pulse is moving too fast in my throat. I should stop doing this. I know it's a bad idea. But it's the only thing that's felt good in weeks.

I wish you could come with me to this thing, Charlie finally writes back. *I could use the company.*

Not sure I'd make good company right now. I'm basically a campaign bot. I've forgotten how to talk to normal human beings about normal human topics.

You've always been good company to me.

They're still just words on a screen. But also all that I have right now. Is he being sweet and serious? Is he remembering my hips pressed against his in a hotel bed? Is he considering what he said to me in the doorway the next morning?

The motion-detecting lights in the office go off, and I stand up with a frustrated groan to turn them back on. This is torture.

I don't respond, and my texts go quiet as I pack up my things to leave. I don't hear from him while I wash my dinner dishes, or as I try to decompress with the help of a jade roller before bed. The silence feels off, like I ended the conversation too early, even though our communication pauses all the time. Finally, I send, *Did you make it out of bed or should I send help?*

Charlie responds with a picture of a bar somewhere. Even through the screen, I can tell that it's dark and loud.

Let me know when you finally get some sleep, I say.

I feel needy, but when I wake up, I have a text from him: *Good night.*

XVII

All the talking has prepared me to see him again, I tell myself. But when Charlie's car pulls up in front of the fundraiser venue, my pulse starts to hammer against my chest. He emerges in pieces, or maybe I just can't take him in all at once, so instead I see hand, wrist, forearm, all tanner than last time. The rolled-up edge of a white oxford shirtsleeve and then his undone collar. The hollow of his throat, the stubble starting to come in after a day of travel. The bow of his mouth. He tugs off his sunglasses and grins at me. "I didn't expect a personal greeting."

Like I was going to miss this. "You're VIP," I remind him.

He puts the sunglasses back on and Blue Steels at me. He's kidding around, but you wouldn't know it from the beads of sweat forming on my breastbone.

"Ridiculous," I say—to myself as much as him.

Charlie wipes his forehead. His shirt pulls up a few inches, and I catch the tan there too.

"I have a surprise for you."

"A surprise?"

He's visibly excited, and I worry I've set expectations too high. "It's silly. Just a little thing."

Charlie gives me a small, tender smile, and my stomach does its customary roller-coaster drop.

I start leading us inside so that I don't do anything regrettable. Charlie matches my pace. Up close, I catch his now-familiar scent—sandalwood and something heady and spicy.

I use conversation to force the thoughts out of my mind. "What did you end up reading on the plane?" That's what we were texting about yesterday: the selection of paperbacks at Hudson News.

"This book about buying things—big things. And what we're trying to own when we do," he says. "It's by Eula Biss? I'll give it to you when I finish."

The intimacy of touching his dog-eared pages—I have to switch gears. "When the campaign ends, I will remember how to read a book."

I must sound as beaten down as I feel, because Charlie pauses and turns to face me. "How are you doing?"

How am I doing? Frustrated. Exhausted. I got an *LA Times* reporter to agree to do a story centering UBI and featuring a mayoral candidate who ran on a similar platform in Stockton . . . only to have it fall through because Teresa couldn't—wouldn't?—make herself available for an interview. We need the kind of win that we just can't seem to find, and I'm starting to worry that my role in the campaign depends on making one happen soon. But if I start to say any of that now, I'm afraid I won't be able to stop. And we have a long day ahead of us. And I have months to go after that. So instead I settle for, "I'm OK. It's just an especially stressful phase of a stressful job. I'll get through it."

Charlie's eyes travel across the features of my face, but he doesn't push it. "OK," he says.

When we start walking again, the back of his hand brushes against mine as we pass through a narrow hallway. The contact shoots sparks up my arm. I wonder if it was intentional. If he's thinking about not touching me as intently and intensely as I'm thinking about not touching him.

In the greenroom, I hand Charlie a tote bag and look away while he peers inside.

"Wait. Is this what I think it is?"

"It's not an original. But Kate made a special edition for you. She says you can send her a Char sweater in exchange, if you want."

Charlie holds his *I Am a Fan of Mischief* shirt up to his chest, preening. "I'm wearing this tonight."

Before I can avert my gaze, he's stripping off the button-down he was wearing. He's unselfconscious in the way you can only be if you grew up doing backstage quick changes, and I can't help surveying him. He's thinned out from touring all summer, but the flex of his arms as he pulls the new shirt over his head is the same. The hair on his chest has lightened up in the sun—when did he have time for this sun? I'm jealous of . . . I'm jealous of not knowing, of not being there for it.

Charlie is shaking his hair back into place when Teresa and her chief of staff walk in. "Oh, good," Teresa says, instead of *Hi* or *How are you?* "Maya, they need you in the press room. The reporter from the *Globe* wants a plus-two."

"We're at capacity." We have been for months. Charlie got an up-and-comer from his label—"the next Olivia Rodrigo"—to agree to play too, and then she went viral on TikTok.

"You tell her that," Teresa says firmly.

This is a job for a press liaison—maybe a press liaison's assistant. But it's pretty clear that Teresa doesn't want Charlie and me hanging out—we're back in that place again, now that the new-car sheen of Charlie's endorsement has worn off. "Of course," I say.

I sort out the *Globe* reporter, a former Mischief fan hoping to sneak a couple of friends in who is happy to settle for an autograph. Once I'm in the press room, though, everyone has a question for me, some little something that they want me to weigh in on. I'm glad that I've made myself accessible; I always hate when senior people on campaigns act like they're above this. But as the clock ticks on, I wonder if my time with Charlie is up—if those were my fifteen minutes, before he goes back to living on the screen of my phone.

I only catch a glimpse of him once. The doors have been open for half an hour, and the venue is starting to feel full, humming with chatter and excitement. I'm trying to entice a donor whose daughter I know from college into a conversation with Teresa. Charlie is by her side.

He's still wearing the shirt, and he looks charmingly out of place in a sea of DC business casual. I'm hoping to pass this donor off to Teresa and grab Charlie in the exchange, but it's like she can see what I'm planning as soon as we get close. "Maya, thank you for bringing me exactly who I wanted to see!" she crows. "Elise Willis was just asking about Davidson going negative, and what our response should be—can you go fill her in on your thinking?"

"Of course!" Elise is also a big donor, and extremely skeptical about the direction I've taken the campaign. I highly doubt that she's interested in anything I have to say. *I brought Charlie here. I helped you*, I think. But aside from our thirty-second exchange at dinner, Teresa treats me like I can't be trusted to know what's best for her—or my career. The helicopter-bossing makes me feel like a toddler, and I stalk away before a tantrum can take root.

It feels like forever before Teresa climbs on stage to give her stump speech. I consulted on the draft, and I've heard it so many times I could recite it from memory.

So when we get to the "New Initiatives" section, I know what's coming. *I'm not afraid of big ideas, because big ideas lead to big changes. I'm talking about big ideas like universal preschool. Big ideas like starting a city bank. And big ideas like universal basic income.*

Except that's not what Teresa says. She mentions the preschools. She calls out the city bank. And then she skips right over UBI.

What. The. Fuck. I've been having my doubts about Teresa recently, but I never expected anything as public and blatant as dropping UBI from her speech *without even telling me*.

I slip out as quietly as possible and make my way to the bathroom. I lock myself in the stall and lean my forehead against the cool metal door.

It's possible that she just forgot. It happens, sometimes. The candidate is on autopilot and jumps over a line without meaning to.

It's been hours since lunch, and I can't tell if the ache in my stomach is because I'm hungry, tired, frustrated, or all three. Tears build, but I blink them away and press the heels of my hands over my eyes harder than I need to. Now is not the time.

I hear Charlie's name boom over the loudspeakers. I am not missing his performance to sulk. I set my jaw, unlock the door, and catch myself in the smudged mirror from a distance. I look fine. Not good, but *fine*. Presentable enough to do my job.

I slip into the side door of the venue right as Charlie is launching into the opening chords of "Longer Gone." My body wants to draw forward, to be as close to the sound and to him as possible, but I force myself to plant my feet and cross my arms like I'm merely the political operative I'm meant to be. His voice live is so much *more everything* than it is on a recording—expansive and intimate at the same time. It echoes around me, vibrates through my bones. All of my anxiety and anger from earlier fall away.

The next song is "Sky at Night," the new album's second single, and the crowd eats it up, like they've been waiting for this as long as I have. I'm expecting him to close with a Mischief song—their debut single, a much-beloved pop song called "Trouble Comes."

I'm not expecting the other three members of Mischief to walk out and join him on stage to do it.

The four of them haven't been seen together since they broke up more than fifteen years ago. They certainly haven't performed together. Instantly, I'm fifteen again, feral at the sight of Ramsey running out on stage, pumping his fists, followed by Chris breaking out his movie-star grin . . . and then, reluctantly, Devin. I let out a scream of joy so fierce it takes me by surprise. But then I catch the eye of a woman near me—about my own age—looking like she's having her own religious experience, and we make the Mischief "M" hand signal at each other and laugh at ourselves.

"I brought some old friends for this one," Charlie says, as pleased with himself as we are with him, and I want to kiss the smirk right off his face. If there was ever a way to get people to hear Teresa's name, hosting a surprise Mischief reunion is definitely it.

When they launch into the song, my whole body goes helium-light. It's impossible not to love them just like I always have, to experience their music like it's part of me. Their harmonies have shifted and changed, but their voices still sound right together. They aren't exactly as they once were, and I like them just as much.

When they walk off stage, I'm beaming and beelining for the greenroom—I have to thank Charlie. To say hi to the rest of them. My god, if Kate flipped about having Charlie at her wedding, she's going to lose her mind about me meeting Ramsey.

But before I can get there, Teresa cuts me off and redirects me toward some donors. She keeps me by her side for the next hour. I can practically feel the tug of my leash, but I don't fight it. Of course this is happening. *Of course.*

By the time I make it to the greenroom, I know it's going to be empty. That I have to grab my bag where I dropped it when I arrived this morning just adds insult to injury.

But there he is. Charlie, sitting on a couch, his book in his lap. He's still wearing that stupid shirt. He looks up and smiles at me, and something very, very dangerous happens in my chest.

"Hey," he says. "Everyone else took off, but I thought I'd stick around for a minute. See how you fared."

My legs carry me without my brain's input. I flop down next to him on the sofa, my eyes falling closed as soon as my ass hits the cushion. "I'm here."

"Do you need coffee? A shot?"

"A shot," I mumble, lids still shut. If I open them, I'll have to acknowledge where I am and what I'm doing. At least shift so we aren't inches away from each other, my thigh sliding perilously close to his. So I can't tell that some of his cologne wore off while he was performing, and he smells even better now.

I hear the rustle of cloth on cloth, and for a second, I think he's reaching for me. I go fever-hot, anticipating his touch. But then the cushion underneath me moves as his weight shifts and he stands up.

I open my eyes and see him standing over me. "C'mon," he says. "Whiskey next time. You should probably get to bed."

Next time. The promise of there being a next time should be enough, but the way my stomach drops at the impending goodbye brings into focus just how much I managed to get my hopes up in the last ninety seconds. I've been on my feet for the last fourteen hours. I'm drunk with exhaustion, and with the sight of him. All of my self-control has been used up, and I want to do what I want for the first time today. "Can't we have just one drink first?"

XVIII

We head to a dive bar, the kind of place no one will be looking for former boy banders or disgraced politicos. I crawl into a booth, and Charlie fetches our drinks. A genuine nightcap, with no professional pretext.

"I don't even want to know what you had to say to Devin to get him out here."

Charlie laughs. "No, you really don't. But you *should* know I have a silent meditation retreat in my future."

He rolls the ice around in his glass, and I sense he's giving me an opening to share more. Instead, I mimic his gesture.

He clears his throat. "What happened with Teresa's speech?"

I don't want to talk about that here, now. To taint the time we have together. "I'm . . . honestly not sure."

He settles back in the booth, tilting his head from side to side, stretching his neck. I could watch it all day. When we were just texting, I could keep things compartmentalized. I could try to pretend Charlie was just another friend. In person, I can't.

"Have you ever thought about doing what she does?" Charlie asks. "Being the candidate yourself?"

I close my eyes again and shake my head.

"Never?"

"I don't want the pressure. Or the compromises. I watch what people have to put up with, and the deals they have to make. Even people who are decent coming in . . . politics almost always breaks them. I want to spare myself from that." I've given some version of this response for years, but as I recite it now, I can't actually tell how it differs from my current reality.

"Yeah." Charlie stretches his legs out as much as he can in our cramped booth. Our knees knock together once, and then again. I have to concentrate on what he's saying when he speaks. "It's been really interesting, reentering this world as an adult. The whole 'being famous' thing, I mean. You were right. It helps being older."

He looks down at the glass in his hands. "I told myself I was getting back into it for the music—for the creative outlet that I had with Char at the beginning, before it became a full-blown business. But I like the travel, and the excitement. I like hearing my music on the radio again. I do like the celebrity." He pauses. "And I hate myself a little for that."

He's absentmindedly drumming his fingers on the table, and without thinking, I reach over and rub my thumb across his knuckles. His hand stills, and then he angles it up and threads his fingers through mine. Our knees are still touching. If we sat here all night, I think I would eventually end up in his lap. "I mean, I told you this in LA—I do like the power this job gives me. I try to use it for good, but . . . I can't help liking it. And anyway." I take a deep breath. Smell stale beer, the smoke of my whiskey, and him. "We all want to be seen."

"I want a lot of things." Charlie's gaze locks on mine, and my pulse thrums between my legs in response.

"Like what?"

I've been holding back as best I can. I've been the very best and brightest professional version of myself for months. I've been obedient and quiet and nearly flawless in the service of someone else's dream. Now I want to be base again: to get my hands on Charlie's skin and scratch marks into its smoothness. To be wet and wrecked underneath him. I flip our linked hands over and circle my thumb in his palm. I take my lip between my teeth. It's barely a decision.

"Maya," Charlie says. His eyes bounce between my thumb and my mouth.

My limbs tingle. The silence between us is heavy and full.

"I thought we couldn't."

I nod slowly, thoughtfully, but my intention is clear. "It would be *better* if we *didn't*." It feels so good to stop lying to him. To stop lying to myself.

His bottom lip drops, just slightly, and I watch his breath catch. He leans forward and murmurs, "Better for who?"

I'm honestly not sure anymore. Me? Teresa? Him? Nobody? Everybody? I force myself to pull away, put my palms on the table and think this through for at least thirty seconds. "I still can't afford to have this be the story. It can't . . . it can't be anything more than tonight." One more indulgence before I give him up for good.

His knee shifts away from mine. He looks distracted, like he's weighing his options, and my stomach drops. If I have to go home alone, after everything—Teresa, and then this—

But then he shakes his head ruefully. "I can't say no to you, Maya."

"Don't."

I drive us back to my apartment, exactly ten miles over the speed limit. When we get there, I don't bother to turn the lights on as I lead him straight back to my bedroom.

Time slows down the moment he touches my waist and pulls me to him. I try to memorize every sensation: his calluses against my collarbone as he unbuttons my shirt, the linen of the bedspread cool and smooth under my bare back as he pushes me onto the mattress and climbs on top of me. His mouth against my stomach as he tugs down my skirt. How his eyes widen when he sees that I put on lace underwear this morning, hoping against hope for exactly this moment.

Before, we had the false promise of time. Now we have urgency. He uses one hand to reach behind his head to pull off his T-shirt, and he unbuttons his pants with the other. I pull him toward me, but he slows me, his hands over mine, just long enough to grab a condom from his pocket—a condom I let myself believe he put there this morning—before we tug off his pants and underwear together.

Now I push him to seated and straddle him, just short of panting. He watches, eyes bright and serious, as he presses his fingers inside of me, so slow, so achingly fucking careful.

His head falls, heavy, against my shoulder. "God," he murmurs. "God, you feel so good already."

I want him to keep talking, but I'm also afraid of the words spilling out of his mouth. Afraid of how much he might mean them. And afraid that if I don't stop him now, I never will.

So I wrap my legs around his hips and pull him to me. Charlie grunts in response. His thumb reaches down to circle my clit, making me shake with each little turn. "Maya," he says. "Can I—"

The answer is yes, always yes. I kiss him. I spread my knees wider. We both gasp as he sinks in and in and in.

I throw my head back, bare my throat. Charlie's hands are tight on my hips as he fucks me, and suddenly it's all too much, too emotional, too real. I have to close my eyes against the image of him, his bare chest, his whole body working. I let myself white out into sensation. I'm so overcome that my orgasm takes me by surprise. It rips through me, almost violent. I realize too late that my teeth are on Charlie's shoulder, that I'm leaving bite marks as he comes.

We collapse on our sides on top of my comforter, and I lie boneless.

"Thanks," I say, when I can find my voice again. "That was . . . what I needed." *You are what I need*, I don't dare say.

He laughs. "I'm glad." He rolls onto his back and looks over the wrecked spread of my body. I'm just starting to feel self-conscious when he lifts a hand and brushes a lock of sweaty hair off my forehead. "I know this is none of my business, but . . . if you want to leave the campaign, you can leave. You know that, right?"

I shrug, moving just slightly away from his touch. Easy for him to say; for him, working is optional at this point. Plus, I *love* this work. Maybe not this campaign, but this campaign isn't forever. I can't let my experience of it stand between me and the rest of my career. I'm so close to being done with it. And *then* I can do what I want.

"It's not that bad," I assure him. "You witnessed a weird night." I think he can tell I'm brushing him off.

"You just . . ." he sighs. "You should be allowed to have a personal life."

"I have a personal life."

"But you know what I mean, Maya. One you don't have to hide. Teresa is happy to have me around the campaign. Would it really be so much worse to have me around you too?"

A hot rush of tears presses, suddenly, angrily, against the backs of my eyes. I've wondered that exact same thing, and every time, I've shoved the possibility away. Even if Teresa were to somehow magically be cool with it, the rest of the world cares *a lot* about Charlie, and somehow just as much about me and Charlie together. It would put me back in a spotlight I've been trying desperately to avoid.

I'm ashamed to admit it, but I might be more scared of me and Charlie than Teresa is.

I overcompensate. "I think maybe you don't get the ways in which your experience of public attention has been very, very different from mine. You are famous. I am infamous. Your *Vogue* profile was a victory lap—mine was crisis PR. This is my life," I say, a little too crisply. "And my job. And I can't take more pressure on either of them, and I can't—don't want to—run away from them."

I've gotten so used to being ruthless with myself, but it feels awful to inflict that on Charlie. That detached, cruel voice sounds much uglier out loud.

Maybe it's for the best. Emotional distance and distrust have become a part of who I am, and Charlie would figure that out eventually. Might as well be now.

Charlie stretches out on his back and looks up at the ceiling.

"I have a super early flight tomorrow. My alarm is set for three a.m.," he says. "I should head back to my hotel. Let you sleep."

No, no, no. Stay. Tell me you see through me. That you want my problems to be your problems.

But I've already asked him for so much. I can't expect more. "That makes sense," I say, eyes on the ceiling as well.

Charlie pats the bed and sits up. The only light in the room is filtering in from outside, framing him in faint, grainy yellow. I can't believe I'm not doing everything in my power to keep him here.

I watch as he gets dressed, slipping into his pants, carefully folding the T-shirt I gave him, and digging his now-creased collared shirt from his bag. I let a tear slide down my cheek as he quietly lets himself out.

XIX

On Monday at the office, Teresa makes her excuses to me. UBI is still important to her; they just wanted to test a version of the speech without mentioning it explicitly. Her values are the same. She's still planning on trying to get a pilot going when she's elected. She's so grateful for all of my help.

Normally I would consult with Gabe about this, but he was the one who brought me onto the campaign in the first place. I don't want to complicate things for him. I consider calling Kate, but I know exactly what she'll say—to trust my gut. Leave if I feel like leaving! Which is so Kate, so California, and something I'm so not in the position to do. Besides, I didn't handle it particularly well when Charlie suggested the same, and I don't need to risk damaging another relationship.

It's September. Two more months. If I bail now, that'll be its own story—that I've become a prima donna. Too emotional, too difficult to work with. That I'm not worth the trouble.

Just wait it out. I repeat it like another mantra.

I don't hear from Charlie for the whole week. Which is fair—I know the olive branch is mine for the offering. But I don't know how to, and I don't have a better answer than the one I already gave him. I still can't stop thinking about it. About him. My thoughts loop and tangle. I'm anxious all the time; I wake up with my jaw clenched, hands in fists.

Finally, I decide to get it over with. I spend my walk home the following Monday trying to find something lighthearted and casual to say. I finally settle on capturing the view across the Potomac, where kayakers are watching dusk fall. *Made it out before sunset. What's your jet lag status?*

He doesn't respond that night. I give in and look up his Instagram, which informs me that he's in New York, attending an awards show. He's in my time zone, he's awake, but (I rationalize) he's probably too busy to check his phone.

I go to bed that night with a rock lodged in my throat. When I wake up in the morning, it's still there. And there's still no response.

One day goes by, and then two. When I've finally decided to let it go—stopped checking my phone every thirty seconds, hoping I just missed the notification—I get a reply.

Hey, he says. *I've been trying to figure out how to say this for a while now, but . . . I guess I wasn't ready.*

I brace as he types.

I like you. Too much for things to be casual between us. I know you don't want more and I get it and I'm sorry for pushing you in ways that were probably unfair. But I can't be friends, and I can't be whatever this is either.

I'm at a coffee shop, picking up a latte on my way to work. I don't even make it to the last sentence of the text before my vision blurs with tears. I blink hard, trying to keep them from falling, but there's nothing I can do. My stomach swims with guilt and shame.

I want to yell at my phone. *How was I supposed to know this meant this much to you if you're just telling me now? And what am I supposed to do with this information?*

I slip out of line and dip into the bathroom. It's sterile and utilitarian, a terrible place to break down. The sink drips steadily. That just makes me sob harder.

I cry about Charlie, but, while I'm at it, I cry about Cooper, still, and about Teresa and my frustration with politics, and how scared I am that I'll never work again, or be in love again. Never get anything else right in my life again. I was a prodigy, but I've used up my luck and talent, and this is me now: leaning against a handicap rail, next to a toilet paper dispenser, weeping.

I wrap my arms around myself and lean my forehead against the cool tile of the wall. I think of the last time I did this, just over a week ago. I'm tempted to call out of work, but we're supposed to get a new set of poll numbers in today, and my absence would be glaring. Plus, I'm not sure being alone with my thoughts is the right idea for me. Work was my refuge once. It can be my refuge again now.

So I pull myself back as best I can. Wash my face in the sink. Press a cold paper towel against my blotchy chest. Head into the office.

My mind spins up useless advice the whole way there. *Text him back. Say you're sorry. Leave him alone; he doesn't want to hear from you. Get yourself together.* And one thought, over and over and over again: *How did you think this was going to end?* I'm so deep in it that I get into an elevator at work without realizing Gabe is already standing there, holding the doors open for me.

"You OK?" he scans me. "You look a little . . ."

"Fine," I say. "Allergies."

"Sure. Well, I actually have good news that might help with your 'allergies.'" He gives the most theatrical air quotes I've seen in my life. "I think we're gonna owe Charlie a gift basket."

I try to say something—anything—but I'm still shaken up, and what comes out is a garbled half-laugh, half-sob. As we arrive at our floor, Gabe hits *door close*. "Maya. Come on. I've seen you look more pulled together at two a.m. at a frat party."

I'm mostly cried out, but I still don't have it in me to give him a real laugh. God*damnit*. "I'm fine. Don't worry about it. Why do we owe Charlie?"

Gabe shakes his head and hits the button for the ground floor. The elevator starts to descend. I'm still miserable, but getting a little distance from the office does make my stomach hurt just slightly less.

"I'll text Teresa and tell her I'm briefing you," he says. "We can meet with her about the numbers after, if you're up for it."

"You really don't have to. I'm OK; I just need a minute."

"Neither of us have seen sunlight in weeks. Let me take a little walk with you, OK?"

Gabe holds out an arm, and I tuck myself underneath it, leaning my head against his chest. We used to walk home from parties this way in college sometimes, drunk and exhausted, holding each other up. I've forgotten, recently, that we were friends long before we were colleagues.

I let Gabe steer me to a coffee shop down the block and get me the latte I failed to buy, plus a chocolate chip cookie. It's not very good, but I eat all of it anyway, suddenly ravenous.

"Now," Gabe says when I'm down to the crumbs. "What's going on?"

I close my eyes. It's so humiliating to admit that I'm heartbroken, especially when it's not even from a full-fledged relationship—and when it's my own fault. "Charlie."

"Well, obviously"

Now I can at least laugh.

"Teresa still being Teresa?"

That's part of the problem, but I don't want to explain the rest. I give him a look, and he laughs back. "OK, fair enough."

"Gaaabe. What do I *do*?" I whimper, conjuring my best love-lorn teenager.

"Listen, best of luck to you if you take the advice of a guy whose boyfriend recently dumped him for working too much, but: it is just work."

"Do you miss him? Aaron?"

Gabe looks past me, out the window. Fall has already turned the leaves, the days keep getting shorter, and it's hard not to feel like the whole world is running out of time.

"Of course I do," he says. "But I think that ship has sailed, and I'm not a strong enough swimmer to chase after it. So I'm distracting myself with the numbers. They're good, Maya. They're really good. *We could win this thing* good."

Whatever this is with Charlie is a mess I don't know how to see my way out of. Work is concrete. Controlled. Life with

Charlie would be a risk, a leap. Here, the ground is solid under my feet.

I take out my phone and type a response to Charlie.

I wish I knew how to make it work. I'm sorry for pushing you too.

XX

Election day dawns bright and frigid. I wake up before my alarm and stare at the ceiling of my Boston hotel room, unable to fall back asleep or make myself get out of bed.

Teresa's poll numbers have been inching up ever since the fundraiser, and we're in really good shape at this point. Better than anyone expected. But it's still not a sure thing. It never is, until someone concedes.

Part of me is proud—the ambitious, striving, *I'll show them* part. It's clear that the work I did on this campaign made a difference. And I believe with everything in me that Teresa is a better candidate than her opponent.

But she's never fully recommitted to UBI after backing off during the fundraiser. It's still on her website, and she touts her "groundbreaking economic ideas" in speeches. But she never calls it by name anymore.

If I was a better politico, I'd appreciate that she read the tea leaves. Dropped something that wasn't getting her the coverage she wanted and traded it for other things that were. It's still possible that she'll push through the pilot if she's elected.

Still, when I finally throw off my covers and get up to brush my teeth, it's with more resignation than excitement.

There isn't much left for me to do at this point. Our social and media teams have their marching orders; occasionally I get a text from someone asking for clarification on a talking point, but otherwise, I'm watching everyone else run around and worry.

It's early evening by the time I accept the fact that my work here is done and put in my headphones to scroll TikTok. I keep trying to convince the algorithm to stop serving me Charlie content, but unfortunately, it knows my soul, and of course today, on election day, the barrage is worse than ever. I'm flooded with images of him performing at the fundraiser, lips grazing the mic. He looks *so good*, even in a wobbly recording, and I remember the way he felt, sitting across from me in a booth that night. Resting a hand on my shoulder at the hotel bar in LA. The first time he pulled me in for a kiss, and the last time too.

I get so swept up in nostalgia for my not-so-distant past that it takes me a few minutes to grasp what I'm being served next: video after video of girls and women giving first-person testimonials to the camera. Talking about how Charlie's advocacy encouraged them to look up UBI or saying they registered to vote at his concert over the summer. His activism isn't the center of his persona, but ever since he committed to the press conference, he's been dedicated to using his voice.

To being brave. To *trying*.

There's a tap on my shoulder and I look up to see Gabe standing over me. "Another set of exit polls just came in," he says, anxious and excited in equal measure.

Five hours later, I'm in the room watching Teresa take a call from Davidson, conceding the race. This is always one of those moments that makes the work worth it. The catharsis of victory. Watching the candidate realize that the campaign is really over and seeing her stride onto the stage and tell a room full of exhausted, fidgety people that all of *their* hard work has paid off. This one night when power tips from one hand into another, and it really seems that change is possible.

I haven't had a sip of alcohol all night, but as Teresa starts her victory remarks, I accept a plastic flute of champagne and down it in three swallows. All around me, people are hugging and cheering, holding back tears.

I don't feel energized or even relieved. I feel . . . hollowed out. Almost like I used to when I turned in my last paper for the semester. Walked out of a final. *That was hard, but I did it. Now I'm free.*

Free from what, to do what? I have no idea.

Teresa finds me when she comes down into the crowd. "We did it, Maya!" she crows.

"We did!"

She holds me at arm's length and smiles. It's the warmest she's been toward me in months. "I know it wasn't easy for you," she says. "Do you know Richard Wilson's considering a run at the next New York Senate race? He asked if I'd put you two in touch."

Richard Wilson is young, but he's already angling for a go at the presidency when it's time. Aligning my name with his—guiding him toward that goal—would likely erase any lingering association with Cooper and make my name my own again. He's not that exciting to me politically: another man with a Rhodes scholarship, a JD from Yale, and milquetoast liberal politics.

"I would love that," I tell Teresa. I'm not sure what else there would be to say.

XXI

I fly back to DC the next morning and spend the rest of the day in bed, alternating between sleeping and watching a *Real Housewives* marathon. On Thursday I finally emerge from my cocoon and realize that there is basically nothing—not even coffee—left in my apartment.

When I open my door, showered and resigned to a windy trudge to a coffee shop, there's a package sitting in the hallway for me. Small, plain, brown. Its return address is a jewelry brand in New York, one I know but have never bought from.

I take it back into my apartment and open it. A small black box sits in a nest of tissue paper, accompanied by a note.

Maya,

I know all the reasons I shouldn't send this, and I'm sure you do too. But I saw it and it made me think of you—a reminder that the world doesn't always end when you think it will.

Congratulations on the win.

Charlie

I press the paper to my chest, just briefly, before setting it aside and opening the lid. A necklace with a charm at its center: a snake, winding into an infinity sign, with a stone set on its head. Something twisted but not tangled. Sinuous and strong; whole and complete.

I sweep my hair away from my neck and fasten the cord, the pendant falling into place right beneath my clavicle. I'd been optimistic that after thirty-six hours of bed rot I'd have gained the ability to start processing things again—especially things with Charlie. But the gift is so unexpected that it sets me back to a place of utter confusion.

In a daze, I reorient myself toward the quest for caffeine. On the walk, I can't stop touching the necklace, its metal warming by degrees from sitting against my skin.

I'm so distracted that I'm not really looking where I'm going. I open the café door and collide with the woman who's leaving as I'm coming. Her coffee tumbles out of her hands and spills at our feet. For a second, all I see is a flurry of blonde hair and big blue eyes, wide and surprised.

Then her face registers. Cassidy.

The woman Cooper cheated with.

"Oh, fuck," she says, looking around frantically for a napkin. A barista rushes over and hurries us out of the way, bringing over a mop to deal with the mess.

I'm paralyzed, too stunned to think or feel or move. *Get out of here*, I command myself. *LEAVE.* But my legs won't move.

Cassidy stands up and looks at me. It happens in slow motion when she recognizes me too.

I only met her a few times, before. She was a low-level DC intern on Knight's presidential race, and I was traveling a lot, by his side more often than not. Apparently, Coop would come by the office looking for me sometimes. Apparently, that's how they met.

The image of her burned into my brain is the photo the newspapers used. They'd pulled it from her socials, obviously, and it was taken during a party. Her mouth was pink and glossy, her cheeks rosy and full. She was wearing a tube top that showed a slice of flat, tan stomach. Even though I tried not to look too long or too hard, it was impossible not to see that she seemed young and fun in precisely the way that I, a woman at that point drowning in professional responsibilities, was not.

Now, though, she's thinner. Muted. Her face is bare, eyes dark-circled. She can barely meet my gaze.

"I'm sorry," she says, in the smallest possible voice.

"It was my fault. I wasn't looking where I was going."

"I don't mean about—" Cassidy starts.

"I'm better off without him." My body is finally functioning again, so I step to the side, attempting to brush by her, but Cassidy grabs my arm.

Her voice is more certain. "No, listen, I'll let you go in a sec, but I promised myself if I ever saw you I would say—I'm so sorry. I didn't mean to—it was so stupid. I wish I could take it back." She laughs a bitter little laugh. "I mean, you already knew this. But he wasn't worth it."

She doesn't look like a villain. She looks like any other Georgetown senior who I might spend half an hour with, talking about their future, assuring them that it will all work out. Maybe that's why I say, "I do know that. Listen, do you—can I buy you another coffee?"

She eyes me suspiciously, then shrugs. "I couldn't afford the first one, really. So sure."

We sit together at a café table by one of the windows. The paranoid part of me knows that it's a bad idea, and the rest of me is too tired to care. Teresa won her campaign, just like Knight won his. The argument that I'm a liability is losing ground.

In fact, I might be the last one who believes it.

"How's it been for you?" I ask once we're settled.

Cassidy shrugs. "Awful. But it's my fault. I should have known better."

I remember the first time someone accused me of sleeping my way to the top. I was younger than Cassidy is now. Twenty, maybe twenty-one. A college intern on my first presidential campaign. Trying desperately to impress anyone and everyone. Of course I stayed late when one of the field managers asked me to. We spent a couple of hours talking strategy. Ate some mushy takeout burritos. He told me I was smart, and I glowed with the compliment. He didn't even make a move on me.

But then word got around that we'd been in his office alone at 9:00 p.m., and everyone assumed what they assumed. I had never felt so foolish.

Cassidy actually did what she's been accused of. But the truth is that I had a crush on that field manager. Envied his beautiful, self-possessed girlfriend, who came by sometimes to sit on his desk and chat, bring him a macchiato, or meet him for dinner. If he had asked—if he had wanted—would I have said yes? If he had insisted I wasn't just smart, but pretty too? I remember exactly what it was like to be that young, and to need someone to tell me who and what I was.

I worry I haven't grown out of it yet.

"He should have known better," I say.

Cassidy nods. She looks like she's heard this before, and I'm sure she has. She doesn't seem convinced.

"I saw Teresa Powell won," she says. "Congratulations."

I'm a little surprised she clocked my involvement, but of course she did—I would have if I were her, anyway. I chew on my next question, trying to get it right. "What are you up to?"

Cassidy shakes her head, her smile cynical, too wide. "Who the fuck would hire me?" Then her face drops. "I think I'm gonna move back in with my parents at the end of the month. They're out in Berkeley. I'm less radioactive there. I hope."

It's surprisingly easy to feel for her—to want more for her. "People forget, eventually. And no one cares about DC as much as DC does."

"I guess."

"I know."

"It doesn't feel that way right now. It's hard to imagine a world where this doesn't follow me forever." Cassidy sighs and pulls the sleeves of her sweater down over her hands.

And just like that, any remaining desire I had to punish her—to make her feel guilty—drains out of me. It's replaced by a desire for a second chance, for both of us. "This won't last forever. And in the meantime, you can't let other people's shitty opinions tell you how to live your life. You are not this one thing you did. Or this one thing that was done to you."

As I say it, I believe it. The reason that all the scrutiny I've faced in the last year and a half felt so heavy was because part of me felt I deserved it. I made the stupid decision to marry Cooper, to fall for his charisma and intelligence and overlook the rest, and these were the consequences. But why did total strangers get to weigh in? What right did they have to judge me? And when did I decide I cared what they thought?

As if she can hear what I'm thinking, Cassidy says, "I mean, at least I know who my real friends are now. Some people really show up when the shit hits the fan. But the rest of them . . ."

I nod. I think of Kate, who never asked questions, who flew across the country to be with me. Gabe, who stood by me at parties when I was a pariah and stuck his neck out to get me a job.

Charlie, who wanted me to work with him without question. Who never lectured me, or suggested my baggage was a burden. I reach up and press the necklace where it's sitting under my sweater. I pull out the pendant and roll it between my fingertips.

"That's beautiful," Cassidy says.

"A friend gave it to me, to remind me that the world never ends when you think it will." I laugh. "And I guess it's a reminder both of us could use?"

"Sounds like a pretty good friend," she says, nodding.

"He is," I say. But of course, he's not a friend. He never was.

XXII

I go straight from the coffee shop to Union Station and get myself a seat on the next Acela to New York. I have nothing with me except the things I threw in my bag when I left my apartment this morning—maybe a phone charger, definitely not a change of clothes. I realize I don't even know where Charlie lives.

All I know is that I'm done being ashamed. And I'm done being scared. If I can find people who've loved me through all of this, I can find people who will hire me too. Even if I do end up in another high-profile relationship. Even if it ends badly.

I send Charlie a text: a picture of the view from my window. *If I told you I was on my way to New York to see you . . . would that be flattering or presumptuous?*

He might not agree to see me. He might not respond, ever. And if that's the case, I can't blame him. But I have to at least try.

I settle into my seat and force myself to ignore my emails. Richard Wilson's people reached out this morning, and normally I would already be scheduling a meeting with them. Getting my next gig lined up.

But Richard is exactly the kind of candidate who seems like

he'll be better for my career than for the country. The kind I told Charlie I was done with, after Knight. After Cooper.

I'm not sure yet what I'm going to do next. But it's a relief to think that Wilson isn't my only option. Maybe instead I can look for people I want to work with. Do this on my own terms. And find a role where I'm not meant to hide some part of myself—where I'm allowed to do more than just shut up and sing.

I nod off and wake up to my phone's vibration. Charlie. *I believe the word is audacious.*

Charlie lives in the kind of West Village brownstone that I thought only existed in movies. I stand out front taking in the fading afternoon light, wishing for a warmer coat, and trying to steel myself. It's still possible that he's already closed the door on me, on us. That the necklace was a congratulatory acknowledgment, a professional nod. It's been months since we last talked; I have no idea where his head is, aside from his willingness to send me his address.

I still can't think of a single excuse good enough to keep me from walking up the steps and knocking on the door.

Charlie answers in a pair of sweatpants and a cashmere sweater. His feet are bare, and I don't think I've ever seen him quite like this. *He's home*, I realize. He's letting me see him at home. A rush of warmth and want threatens to overwhelm me. I let myself experience it, turn toward the feeling instead of away. "Hi." Who knew my voice could tremble so much over the course of a single syllable.

"Hi yourself."

As he tries to make sense of me standing there, all of the old familiar fears emerge. That I shouldn't be here. That I'll get myself in trouble. That sensation of being out in the open, exposed. I have the urge to turn my head, to see if anyone is watching us, but I don't. I stay focused on Charlie.

After a moment he nods, and I follow him in.

He leads me down a narrow hallway that opens onto a palatial living room. I pause for a moment to take it all in: the plants, the abstract, colorful art. The fireplace, an honest-to-god fire lit in the grate.

We stand facing each other. Charlie runs a hand through his hair. A log crackles and sighs. I'm pretty sure my body does the same.

"Do you need anything? Water?" he asks.

"I just need to talk."

He gestures toward the couch but settles himself in an arm-chair across from it.

I take a deep breath. I didn't let myself practice my speech on the train; I didn't want to come across as rehearsed, but now that seems silly. I wish I knew exactly what I was going to tell him. That I had any hope of getting this right.

"I want to start by apologizing," I say, wincing inwardly at how much I sound like one of my candidates making a last-ditch speech after a bad gaffe. I take a deep breath and start again. "I'm sorry for getting so wrapped up in my own insecurities and fears that I made such a mess of this. I've been ashamed of myself, because people kept telling me that I should be. And I was dumb enough to believe them, and even dumber to think it meant I wasn't allowed to be happy. Or didn't deserve to be happy. I was trying to be so good that nobody could judge me. I thought maybe that way—" I have to laugh at myself. "Maybe that way, I would be infallible. Impenetrable."

Charlie nods, his face inscrutable. His hands are laid careful and flat on his lap. "I was really mad at you, that night in DC. You wouldn't even—you didn't even want to try."

"I know."

"I just kept thinking—this is special. And you walked away from it." He sighs.

Up until now, I've been maintaining eye contact, making sure he knows how much I mean everything I'm saying. But hearing him put it like that fills me with such regret that it physically hurts. I pinch the bridge of my nose and turn my gaze toward the floor. Take another deep breath.

"When my life was blowing up, I fantasized about a future when I'd eventually regain a sense of control. That night after the fundraiser, when I pushed you away, I was just trying to take the reins of something. It felt like one of the few outcomes I could guarantee in that moment. And I honestly thought I was only hurting myself, which, after everything I'd been through, seemed like pain I might be able to live with. I didn't realize I was hurting you too. Saying it now, I know it sounds nuts, and I can only blame the fact that I had my head shoved very, very far up my own ass. Charlie, I never, ever meant to hurt you, and I have never, ever wanted to be just friends."

He's been containing himself, but he gets up and starts to pace around the room. "You showed up at my door."

"I showed up at your door."

He waits.

I spread my arms out, a gesture of helplessness. "My life imploded. I tried to white-knuckle through it. And I was doing a pretty good job until you—until you."

"That was you doing a good job?"

I suppress a smile. "You're the one who wanted to hire me. You're also the one who made me want to blow up everything in my life, just as I was putting it back together. It scares the shit out of me, Charlie. The only thing that scares me more is the idea of not doing everything possible to be with you."

Charlie shakes his head, but he's smiling, now, like he can't believe he held out this long. "Come here," he says.

I stand to meet him, and he wraps his arms around me and presses his lips to my temple. My muscles take this as their cue to uncoil, to expel the tension they've held for so long, I had forgotten how to notice it.

"When I saw your picture in *Vogue*, I thought you were beautiful," he murmurs. "But when I met you that night at Denizen and you opened your mouth, I thought—*Oh, I'm in so much fucking trouble.*" I tilt my chin up but can't get my mouth to work now. Charlie keeps going. "I can't believe you're here."

With him wrapped around me, I feel only calm. The fears, the anxieties, the self-doubt—I've deprived them of their power. I can't believe I let them dictate my life as long as I did. "I'm going to say something earnest again, OK?"

He laughs.

"This is the first time in a really long time that I'm sure I'm where I'm supposed to be."

"Well, good luck leaving."

"Good luck getting rid of me." I'm still smiling up at him, and finally, finally, he tilts his face down to kiss me. I'm overcome.

And I'm startled when he pulls away.

I open my eyes and see Charlie looking a little too pensive for this moment. Anxiety grips me again. Of course it couldn't be this easy.

He drops his hand from where it was resting on my waist, and now it's scratching the back of his neck, doing that thing he does when he's being thoughtful. "I meant what I said in that text, Maya. I'm not asking for all or nothing, but I'm trying to be more honest with myself these days, more direct about what I want. And the truth is I do want . . . you, and this. I don't have an answer for how to make it work with your life and your job, or my life and my job. But I can't hide or half-ass it while we figure it out."

I nod. "Do you remember what you said to me that first morning after we spent the night together in LA?"

I watch him search for the moment in his memories.

"You told me I could have as much of you as I wanted. And I fucking *swooned*—because it was very sexy. Extremely. But also because it was generous, and brave. Which is what you are. And what I'm still working on becoming." I take a deep breath. "You can have as much of me as you want, Charlie. I mean it."

It's quiet for a moment as he mulls over my words. And then he leans in and kisses me again, slow and deliberate. "I want this," he says, pulling away and tapping a finger on my bottom lip. His mouth moves to my neck, grinning. "And this." My breast. "And this." My hip. "And this."

"All yours," I promise him. "All yours."

This isn't the end. There's more of Maya and Charlie's story to be had: Read the epilogue, listen to "Longer Gone," and get your own Mischief fan club tee and Lizzie Fortunato snake necklace by scanning here or visiting 831stories.com/bigfan.

ACKNOWLEDGMENTS

First of all, thank you to Claire and Erica for inviting me on this adventure with you. Thank you to Kia Thomas for your thorough, thoughtful edits.

Thank you to Dorland Mountain Arts Colony, where I spent a beautiful week and wrote part of an early draft. (And thank you to Mom, Edan, and Kristen for your companionship while I was there!) Speaking of which, thank you, Mom, Dad, and Jordan, for everything, always.

Thank you to everyone else who kept me company throughout the rest of the writing and editing process, including but not limited to Sarah, Maurene, Elissa, Doree, Kate, and Aminah. Should we do a sprint now?

Thank you to everyone who has ever answered one of my texts, particularly the people of Lady Jujitsu, One Direction Study Group, Cody Bellinger Fan Club, Tyrannical Hot Girl Cult, Gorgeous Ladies of Muscle Porch, Chavurah Daughters, and I Would Simply Leave Shadyside.

Thank you to Weetzie Cat, my therapist, and my Lexapro prescription for keeping me relatively sane.

Thank you to boy bands. And most of all, thank you to the girls who have loved them with me.

From 831 Stories: Thank you, romance readers, for your joyful, inspiring fandom and for letting us join in on the fun. We couldn't be more thrilled to be getting in bed with you.

ABOUT THE AUTHOR

ALEXANDRA ROMANOFF is a journalist, a cultural critic, and the author of three novels (under Zan Romanoff), most recently *Look*, which *O, The Oprah Magazine* called "one of the LGBTQ books that will change the literary landscape." She also cohosts the podcast *On the Bleachers*, which examines the intersection of sports and pop culture. Her favorite member of One Direction is Louis Tomlinson. She lives and writes in LA.